I0682729

Other Books By B. Heather Mantler
Committed to Her Enemy
Chenarcor: Adventures of Alex & Toby
Princess or Pirate
A Thief in Search of a Baby
The Best Brownie Recipe
An Adventure for Princess Aurelia
The Prince and the Mermaid
Another Adventure for Princess Aurelia
Joe Tries to Catch a Murderer
Ryan White

Kings of Proster
For Wealth and Glory
Closing the Portal
Mistakes Made
Wasted Love
The Mystery of the Magic
Lovers & Losses
Hillel's Glory
Fighting for the King
The King's Ransom

The Prince of Yester

B. Heather Mantler

Copyright © 2020 Heather Mantler

All rights reserved.

ISBN: 978-1-927507-57-5

To both of them for their support.

VALDA MEETS A MYSTERIOUS PRINCE AND THEY GET TO KNOW EACH OTHER

Valda, the eldest Princess of Proster, smiled at each guest as they entered the ballroom. Each noble her age of Proster were there or coming in, as were many princes from neighbouring kingdoms. Her smile might have dimmed for the princes, but no one seemed to notice. Valda had not really wanted a ball for her sixteenth birthday, but it was pointed out that the visiting nobles needed some entertainment while they were in Proster.

Once everyone was inside, Valda let the guard close the door. She went over to have some punch and worked to avoid anyone who would ask her to dance. Valda knew she would not be successful all evening, but she could try for a few minutes. She made it as far as the refreshments table and got herself the cup of punch before anyone noticed she was not at the door. Offers to dance did not come because of the cup in her hand, but they would if she finished it or put it down.

Valda had hoped to spend her birthday doing a much quieter activity. However, since she had come close to coming of age, the neighbouring kingdoms have been sending their princes under various excuses in case she would pick one and they could become king of Proster when Waldemar passed on. Valda had been raised along with her brother, Aldous, to rule the kingdom, but she felt it likely she would be passed over for the crown. Others did not share that view, so many of the princes were second sons.

The prince of Krastel came over to Valda. He had tried to visit her multiple times since he had arrived, three days ago, and every time she had been able to find some excuse to get away from him. It was not that he lacked in looks, so much as he had an issue with body odour.

"Princess Valda," the prince of Krastel said, "I was wondering if you would do me the honour of dancing with me."

"I have just gotten my cup of punch," Valda said, "Perhaps later."

"Later then," the prince of Krastel said giving a slight bow before moving off. Valda was not sure who he would get to talk with him, but as long as he left her alone. Valda glanced around and spotted a chair beside a post. She managed to sneak over there and sit before anyone else came up to her. Valda watched from her chair.

Everyone was having a good time. They were talking, laughing, eating, and dancing. The nobles from Proster were both male and female, so there was no lack of dance partners. If it was not required for her to be there, Valda was sure everyone would have a good time.

There was a slight scratching sound from the other side of the pillar next to Valda's chair. She listened for a moment before realizing that someone was leaning against the other side. She peeked around the pillar and saw a male about her age. He was wearing a simpler version of what every other male was wearing and seemed uncomfortable in it. His hair was blond and hung down to his shoulders, which was not the current trend. His hands were tucked into his pockets as if he did not know what to do with them. Valda remembered him somewhat from when he had come in, but she had not really had a good look at him then because the prince of Grendal had pushed his way to her and prevented this man from making an introduction.

Valda did not remember seeing him around, so he must have arrived recently. She had heard that several more princes had arrived this afternoon and she would meet them at the ball. She withdrew back to her side of the pillar. Valda sipped her punch and trying to be as small as possible so as not to be noticed. The song ended and many of the couples broke up to find new partners. No one came over to Valda to ask for her to dance, so she felt safe as the new song started. She watched the dancers start twirling around the dance floor.

The man on the other side of the pillar was tapping his foot to the music. Valda kept herself from peeking at him again. She did wonder why he was not dancing if he liked the music so much. Valda did not like dancing even though she could do so passably well. Tonight she lacked any interest in dancing at all, or being around people. There were better uses for her time and energy.

The tapping increased to the beat of the music and slowed down with the beat of the music. The man had excellent rhythm and if he played an instrument he could probably have played along with the musicians. Valda once again wondered why he did not find a partner and dance.

"If you like the music so much, why are you not dancing?" Valda spoke to the pillar.

"Music, I enjoy," the man answered, "Dancing, I cannot do."

"I thought everyone learned to dance these days," Valda said.

"Lessons are not the problem," the man replied, "It is the ability that hinders me from stepping out on to the dance floor. Why are you not on the dance floor?"

"I do not feel like dancing," Valda answered. He did not respond to that and she was quiet for a while. The tapping never stopped.

"What instrument do you play?" Valda asked.

"The flute," the man answered, "As well as any whistle I can whittle. Do you play?"

"No," Valda answered, "I have never had any lessons in the area of music."

"A pity," the man said, "I find it very relaxing and fun."

"You should have brought your instrument," Valda said, "Then you could have joined the musicians."

"I might have, but my chaperone would not let me," the man said, "He feels such behaviour is unbecoming and rude."

"He may be right," Valda said, "But it sounds more like he does not want you to have any fun."

The man laughed, "You are probably right and if I had not promised my parents I would listen to him, I would be having more fun. What do you do for fun?"

"Poetry," Valda answered.

"Reading it or writing?" the man asked.

"Some of both," Valda answered.

"Long poetry or short poetry?" the man asked.

"Both," Valda answered, "Depending on my mood and the poet. Some poets are boring no matter the length of the piece and some who can write great stuff. I prefer those who add humour into their poems."

"And the ones you do not like?" the man asked.

"Depend far too much on abstract imagery or obscure language or are really obtuse," Valda said.

"I can understand that," the man said, "The more you have to search through it for the poet's meaning the harder it is to really get into the poem. Some pieces of music are like that. Those are usually the favourite of music teachers, but the students do not like them."

"Scholars are similar in their favouring the archaic over the simple," Valda said.

The song ended and the tapping stopped. The partners on the dance floor moved on to be partnered with someone else. The prince of Krastel searched the room until he saw Valda and then headed over to her chair.

"Would you do me the honour of dancing with me?" the prince of Krastel asked with a bow.

"I am still drinking my punch," Valda said, "I am sure there is someone else willing to dance with you."

The prince of Krastel seemed as if he wanted to say something more, but instead he bowed again and walked away.

"The library here must be good if scholars come to visit," the man from behind the pillar said.

"It is one of the best in the world," Valda replied, "It is not the largest, but it contains many volumes people say are significant."

"Does it contain the works of Thomas Merritt?" the man asked.

"Both of them," Valda answered.

"I thought he had also produced a third book, which was poetry," the man said.

"He might have," Valda said, "But anything that was not a finished product at the time of his death was burned, so all that is left are the two novels."

"A pity," the man said, "I have read part of one of his books and thought his book of poetry would be interesting to read."

"You have only read part of one book?" Valda asked.

"The library where I come from is small and very limited to those used to teach the basics," the man said, "And the Thomas Merritt book had been dropped in water making most of it unreadable."

"Which book was it?" Valda asked.

"I do not remember the title anymore," the man said.

"Well, come to the library and we can see if we can find it," Valda said.

"Would it not be rude for you to leave the ball?" the man asked.

"They do not need me for another half an hour or more," Valda answered, "It is no problem to be back before then. Come on." Valda stood up and placed her cup on the chair. The man came around the pillar. He was about five foot seven and medium build with eyes of pale green. Valda turned so as not to get lost in them. She worked her way around behind the crowd watching the dancers. The man followed her.

When Valda reached the door, she checked but there was no one paying attention to them. She slipped through and he followed.

"The library is this way," Valda said starting down the hallway. The man kept pace beside her.

"I have not had any time to look around the castle," the man said, "As my chaperone and I only arrived in time to wash up before supper."

"How far did you have to travel?" Valda asked.

"From Yester," the man answered.

"Yester?" Valda said, "Where is that?"

"It is a large island off the North coast," the man answered, "The main industry is fishing and anything else that can be retrieved from the ocean for use."

"That quite the journey," Valda said.

"My parents felt it was necessary," the man said, "I am their only child and with the distance to another kingdom the nobles have become inbred. They had hoped I might bring back a wife."

"And you started here?" Valda asked.

"With instructions to keep visiting kingdoms with females of my age range until I find someone to marry," the man answered, "My mother was a noble from the northern kingdom, who came to Yester because her ship crashed on the shore and she fell in love with my father before they could find a ship to send her back."

"It sounds like not many people leave Yester," Valda said.

"Of the nobility, there are very few who leave," the

man said, "Of the lower classes, people come and go on the fishing ships all the time."

"Nobility has never had much for common sense anyway," Valda said. The man laughed.

"They are known for the lack of brains," the man said.

They reached a door a couple floors up from the ballroom.

"This is the library," Valda said as she opened the door. The man looked around and his expression was suitably impressed. There were lanterns lit all around the room and one placed on a table beside a chair on the other side of the room from the door. In the chair was Valda's brother, Aldous, and he looked up from his book when they entered.

"I was wondering how long before you came up here," Aldous said.

"Well, I was not actually planning to sneak up here," Valda said.

"And this is?" Aldous asked. Valda turned to the man.

"I am sorry, my manners are horrible today," Valda said, "I never got your name."

"My name is Ernest," the man said, "But most people call me Yester because that is where I am from."

"Welcome to Proster, Yester," Aldous said offering his hand, "I am Aldous." Prince Yester stepped forward and shook Aldous's hand.

"Yester has read part of a Thomas Merritt book, but not all of it," Valda said, "And I thought we should see if we could get him a copy he could borrow and finished reading it."

"Which novel are you looking for?" Aldous asked.

"I cannot remember the title," Prince Yester answered.

"I think both of them should be in the library," Aldous said.

"There are over here," Valda said heading into the shelves on the left side. Prince Yester followed her. Valda stopped at one of the shelves and after a minute of searching she pulled two books off the shelf. She offered them to Prince Yester.

"You can borrow them for a while," Valda said, "They are good reads."

"Thank you," Prince Yester said as he looked over the covers. He flipped to the beginning of one book and read the first bit before doing the same to the other book. Then he closed the books.

"I should put these in my room before we head back to the ball," Prince Yester said.

"Of course," Valda said. They headed for the door together.

"Enjoy the ball," Aldous called when they reached the door.

"Good night," Valda called back. Valda and Prince Yester left the library and closed the door behind them.

Prince Yester opened the one book and flipped to the first page again. Valda led the way towards the guest suites, but rather than read to himself, Prince Yester started to read out loud.

"Princess Isadora stood beside the hole where her father's coffin had just been lowered. The rest of the mourners stood behind her. The population of the kingdom was sad King Kenneth was dead as they had prospered under his rule. Princess Isadora was sad that her father was dead, but for different reasons.

While he was ruling the kingdom, no one paid her any attention unless she was needed for official business. Sure, there had been pressure for her to get married and provide an heir. She had wiggled out of every attempt so far. With her father gone, Princess Isadora knew she would not manage to avoid the counsel to be married for very long.

Princess Isadora glanced up from the grave and briefly looked around. She was about to go back to staring at the coffin when she saw the face of a man hiding behind a tombstone. Princess Isadora thought she might have seen him in court the few times she had been forced to attend, but she did not know who he was. He gave her a mischievous grin and then disappeared behind the tombstone. Something about the man made Princess Isadora want to follow him, but she could not get away while she was the centre of attention.

The formalities finally over, Princess Isadora went back into the castle with the rest of the dignitaries. She still could not sneak away, even with the magic ring to turn her invisible. Instead, she ended up at the royal table for lunch. Lord Sterling's son, Medwin, was seated beside her. The others at the table were visiting royalty, whom Princess Isadora did not know as well.

Lunch was as formal as meals could get with all the guests who were there for King Kenneth's funeral. Princess Isadora would have been annoyed at all the stiffness of the occasion, but her mind kept going back to the man in the grave yard. She barely noticed the conversation the rest of the table was having, even when they tried to include her. Only when Medwin elbowed her did Princess Isadora come back to reality.

Everyone in the room seemed to be waiting for her to start eating the main course. Princess Isadora daintily started to eat and then everyone else also started.

Princess Isadora saw the man from the grave yard at a far table. He was sitting with some of the lesser nobles and their families. There was nothing to help Princess Isadora to identify the man. She turned to Medwin, the lord's son everyone seemed to think Princess Isadora would marry.

"That man at the table with Lord Reinhold and family," Princess Isadora said leaning closer to Medwin, "The one with the black hair tied back."

"Yes," Medwin said.

"Who is he?" Princess Isadora asked.

"Wendell's son," Medwin answered.

"I did not realize Wendell had family," Princess Isadora said.

"Most of his family live in a village south of here," Medwin said, "But his oldest son was sent here in hopes that Wendell could stop him from turning into a rogue. From what I have seen of Sprague, he already is a rogue and nothing his father has done has changed him. More things have gone missing after he visits people than at any other time."

Medwin might have gone on about Sprague, but Princess Isadora had stopped listening. Sprague must have noticed someone was watching him because he looked around. He noticed that it was her and he winked before Princess Isadora lowered her eyes to her plate. She was not she why she felt she had to avoid his eyes, so she looked up again. Sprague was no longer there. Princess Isadora looked around but did not see him anywhere."

Prince Yester paused briefly as they started down the stairs, but once he had a rhythm he started reading again.

"Princess Isadora suffered through the rest of lunch with all the stuffy people. Medwin talked to her and did not need her to respond to him, which was fine with her. Some people looked to her as if she was supposed to announce the end of the meal. Medwin had stopped talking to her, so Princess Isadora did what she usually did and got up and left the dining room without any formalities. She could hear mutterings from the dining room as people were not happy with how she was behaving and those people would not have cared what she did last week.

Without thinking about it, Princess Isadora headed for her chambers. She did not get far.

"Princess Isadora," a male voice called to her. Princess Isadora turned to look. It was Lord Stalvey, or as her father had called him Lord Stuckupcis due to the lord being way too formal and finicky.

"Yes, Lord Stalvey," Princess Isadora said.

"When are you going to hold counsel?" Lord Stalvey asked.

"Lord Sterling should have that information," Princess Isadora answered.

"It was always King Kenneth who made the decision as to when it would happen," Lord Stalvey said. Princess Isadora could hear the whine in his voice.

"I am sure if Lord Sterling needs me to choose the date he will ask," Princess Isadora said, "Until then, if you are in a rush talk to him."

"This kingdom is without a king," Lord Stalvey said, "This issue needs to be dealt with immediately."

"I lost my father," Princess Isadora said, "And I need space to mourn him."

Lord Stalvey appeared to be ready to mock her needing space and the thought that she would actually mourn her father, but other people came out of the dining room. Princess Isadora slipped away while Lord Stalvey was distracted.

Princess Isadora hurried up to her chambers to avoid being stopped by anyone else. She succeeded this time. Closing the door, Princess Isadora went to the window. She opened it and sat down on the windowsill. The sun of the afternoon was tempered by a cool wind. Underneath Princess Isadora's window was the gardens and she could smell the flowers.

Afternoons many of the nobility who had nothing else to do would wander the gardens, but not always with people they should be seen with. Princess Isadora did not always care, but occasionally she found news of interest in who walked with whom. Today she really did not care as she just wanted the quiet and the closeness with nature. If she tried to go for a walk in the garden, she would be stopped and everyone would want a word. Some to express their condolences, others to gain gossip, and the rest to pressure her for their benefit.

Movement caught her attention and Princess Isadora turned to look. Sprague was walking in the garden with a girl, Princess Isadora did not recognize. They walked but did not say anything to each other. Princess Isadora figured that Sprague was like every other male in the castle and have a woman on the side. She wanted to cross her arms over her chest and lift her head above him, but she really did not understand why. Sprague was nothing to her, why should she care if he had a woman? Not only that, but she had so much else to think about.

Princess Isadora knew she would be pressured from the court to have a coronation, a marriage, and an heir to the throne. Even Lord Sterling had expressed thoughts on the matter and she had tried to put him off, though she told him that she knew she would have to face those things soon. Princess Isadora wondered who the woman was because she did not remember ever seeing the woman at court. But she had not seen Sprague until today either so who he spends his time with should not matter to her. Nothing Sprague does should matter to her as they have not even been introduced to each other."

Prince Yester stopped reading and stopped walking in front of the door to one of the suites closer to the end of the guest area. Valda stopped as well.

"Thomas Merritt writes so well," Prince Yester said, "I cannot wait to read some more."

"I have read his books several times," Valda said, "And I love reading them again."

"You like tales as well as poetry?" Prince Yester asked.

"Some tales," Valda answered, "Many books are not that interesting. Thomas Merritt, Hadden Grimes, and Aldous are the ones I like best."

"Your brother writes tales?" Prince Yester asked, "He was reading a book on history in the library."

"Aldous has three interests," Valda said, "History, story telling and Theola."

"Theola?" Prince Yester asked.

"That is a long story," Valda said, "Or a really short one, depending on your point of view."

"My tutor loved telling tales," Prince Yester said, "And I took it up because I found it enjoyable."

"Aldous would love to hear your tales," Valda said, "He is always looking for new ones to tell."

"Perhaps sometime tomorrow we can get together and exchange tales," Prince Yester said.

"As far as I know, he has nothing planned," Valda said. Prince Yester smiled at Valda.

"I should put these in my room," Prince Yester said holding up the books. He opened the door and stepped inside. Valda stayed in the hallway.

"You are supposed to be at the ball," a man's voice came from inside the suite.

"I was," Prince Yester replied as he went deeper inside, "And I am about to go back to the ball. I was merely putting these books in my room."

The man might have said something else but he saw Valda standing in the hallway. The man was slightly shorter than Prince Yester with light brown hair and a stoop. His clothing marked him as a servant to royalty. Prince Yester went to one of the rooms and went inside for a mere moment. Then he came back out and to the door. He closed the door as he stepped into the hallway.

"Let us get back to the ball before they miss you," Prince Yester said.

"I doubt they have noticed yet," Valda said, "But I guess we should go back."

"I am guessing that you would rather do something else to celebrate your birthday," Prince Yester said.

"Usually I celebrate with a family supper, a few gifts, and a quiet evening," Valda said, "Many times I go back to reading the same book of poetry every year."

"I would invite you to listen to me read some more,

but the ball will probably end too late," Prince Yester said, "And it would probably be boring for you."

"I accept your invitation," Valda said, "Aldous will go to bed long before the ball is over, so we can meet in the library."

"I will be there," Prince Yester said with a smile. Valda smiled back.

They reached the ballroom again. Valda pushed it open enough to peer into the room. After a moment, she slipped through and Prince Yesterday followed her in. Valda sat down in the chair she had been in before after removing her cup. Prince Yester went back to leaning on the other side of the pillar.

The dancers were still dancing along with the music and people were still watching the dancers. No one appeared to have missed them. Even the prince of Krastel was on the other side of the room talking to someone.

At the end of this song, the musicians took a break. The dancers moved out of the dancer floor and drifted from their partners. The doors were opened and the castle steward along with another servant brought in a cake. Valda got up and accepted the birthday cheers. She cut the cake, passed out the pieces before taking a piece for herself, and sat back down. Everyone was busy eating for a few minutes. Once the cake was eaten, the castle steward brought Valda her gifts. She opened them and thanked those who gave her something. Most of the items were things like jewellery, which she rarely wore what she already owned. There were only a couple of books, one from her parents and the other from Aldous.

After all the gifts were opened and everyone had

been thanked, the people drifted out of the ballroom to go off to their homes or guest suites. Valda stood at the door and bid everyone good bye. Slowly people left. She faked a smile as most of them, but Prince Yester received a real one. When everyone had finally left, Valda went up to her room leaving the servants to clean the mess up or leave it to clean tomorrow.

Valda went to her room to change into something more comfortable than her party dress before heading to the library. She found Prince Yester already there. He was seated in the chair Aldous had been sitting in earlier with the lantern on the table lit. Valda sat down in the chair on the other side of the table.

"You are not too tired to listen?" Prince Yester asked.

"I am used to staying up late reading," Valda answered.

"Okay," Prince Yester said, *"With another sigh, Princess Isadora got to her feet. She left the page on her desk and left her chambers. She used her ring to keep from dealing with anyone else in the castle hallways and avoid trying to answer demands from them. Aside from making sure she did not run into anyone, it was much easier to get through the hallways. When she reached Lord Sterling's office, Princess Isadora looked inside and saw him working at his desk without one else present. She took off her ring before she knocked on the door. Lord Sterling looked and smiled at her.*

"Come in," Lord Sterling said.

"Thank you," Princess Isadora said as she stepped into the office and closed the door. She sat down in the

chair provided for guests.

*"Lord Stalvey was making demands after lunch,"
Princess Isadora said.*

*"He said something to me as well," Lord Sterling
said, "But I suggested he not worry about it. But I
sense the matters bother you."*

*"At the moment, yes," Princess Isadora said, "As
much as I would rather not."*

*"Unfortunately, what we would like is not always
what needs to be done," Lord Sterling said.*

*"My grandfather said that many times," Princess
Isadora said, "But my father never did."*

*"Your father was not necessarily the best at certain
things," Lord Sterling said, "He should have been
training you to rule this kingdom from the moment you
were brought to the castle."*

*"My grandfather did some and asked my tutors to do
the same," Princess Isadora said, "But my father did
not. I think he believed he had plenty of time to teach
me what he thought I needed to know. Because he told
me he would share information on my mother too."*

*"His death was very sudden for all of us," Lord
Sterling said.*

*"I suppose now we need to have a coronation,"
Princess Isadora said, "And then I need to take over
running the kingdom. Then people will demand that I
marry."*

*"I think you will find plenty of pressure for you to
marry starting now," Lord Sterling said, "Anyone who
thinks he had a chance will show up any place you are
rumoured to be."*

*"I will have to remember that before I go
anywhere," Princess Isadora said, "But as far as I*

know there are no rules about me having to marry or there needing to be a king."

"There are no rules of such," Lord Sterling said.

"So, who knows the traditions necessary for a coronation?" Princess Isadora asked.

"I have a book on those," Lord Sterling answered, "I can plan it and set it up. You can pick the day."

"How long does it take to plan one of those?" Princess Isadora asked.

"A few days," Lord Sterling answered, "Though it can be done sooner."

"Few days is fine," Princess Isadora said, "Do we have to wait until after the coronation before having court again, or am I expected to hold it tomorrow?"

"It depends on how you feel," Lord Sterling answered, "If you are ready it can be held tomorrow and if you need more time more time can be given."

"Might be best to get the kingdom back to normal," Princess Isadora said.

"I will let people know," Lord Sterling said.

"Should I be doing that?" Princess Isadora asked.

"You can if you want," Lord Sterling answered, "I am offering to help you get used to ruling the kingdom before you are expected to do everything."

"Okay, I appreciate that," Princess Isadora said, "Any actual help is great because I think there will be plenty of people who claim to help who are not helping me, but themselves."

"As long as you can see that and understand it," Lord Sterling said, "I will do my best to give you the help you need as well as any advice you want. My goal is the best things for the kingdom."

"Then we have the same goal," Princess Isadora

said.

"Remember that goal when things come up that will make you want to rule in favour for yourself rather than the kingdom," Lord Sterling said, "Because there will be times when what you want will not be what the kingdom needs. There were times when your father did not go with what was best for the kingdom, but he knew enough that most of those decisions were not anything that could destroy the kingdom."

"I will do what I can," Princess Isadora said, "My goal is the best thing for the kingdom, but I am not sure I know enough to make the best decisions. I will ask for advice when I need it."

"Good," Lord Sterling said, "Those things show wisdom, so have actions match your words."

Princess Isadora nodded. She remembered too many times when her father said things but there was no action behind them.

"Anything else?" Lord Sterling asked.

"If I marry, he would become king," Princess Isadora said.

"Many would expect so," Lord Sterling said, "But it is not necessarily the result. You could make him consort instead of the king."

"It would be my choice?" Princess Isadora asked.

"Yes," Lord Sterling answered, "Is there anyone you have in mind?"

"No, I was just wondering," Princes Isadora answered, "The pressure for me to find someone will be high and I need to know what are all my options should I find someone I do wish to marry."

"You do not have to give in to pressure from anyone," Lord Sterling said, "But understand that if

you do not provide an heir, one will be chosen from those connected to the royal family by blood."

"That side of the family has been known to dip into the black end of the arts," Princess Isadora said.

"They are," Lord Sterling said.

Princess Isadora nodded to herself again. She understood what Lord Sterling was saying and his warning. It left her with plenty to think about and not much time to really do it. Lord Sterling saw that he had given her things to think about and ponder.

"Any more questions?" Lord Sterling asked.

"No," Princess Isadora answered, "Thank you for everything."

"It is my honour," Lord Sterling said.

Princess Isadora smiled slightly before getting up. She left the door open and started back toward her chambers. Princess Isadora slipped the ring on to avoid having to deal with anyone.

Sprague was surprised to see Princess Isadora disappear, but he had been suspicious of her avoidance of people for the time he had been at court. There were a couple times when he had thought he would run into her in the hallways, but then she had not been where expected. Now he knew that she has something to make her invisible. He would love to have something like that as sneaking around would be much easier, not that he was not good at sneaking around without such.

He moved on as he wanted to get to the kitchens while the cooks were still taking a break from making lunch. The dishwasher never bothered him because he would share his bounty, but the cooks could get mean and might even report him to others who might start

*paying attention to him. Not that there were not some
of those already.*

*Medwin told Sprague that Princess Isadora had
asked about him and Medwin said he was a rogue,
which Medwin knew all too well and used it. Not that
Sprague minded too much. He got favours back from
Medwin at regular intervals for it. He was not sure
what he would ask for after sneaking in Medwin's
girlfriend today, but he was sure he would think of
something. Maybe an introduction to Princess Isadora.
Medwin was considered the Princess's friend and there
was even a rumour they were going to get married.
Sprague knew that was unlikely as Medwin was much
too in love with his girlfriend. The only thing standing
in Medwin's way from marrying her was his father and
Sprague did not know why Lord Sterling was blocking
the marriage.*

*But there were plenty of things that did not make
sense to Sprague since he was forced to move to the
capital. Most of the people around the king were power
hungry but harmless. However, a few were not
harmless, but no one seemed to have noticed that those
were trouble and done anything about them. After
watching King Kenneth rule, Sprague was sure the king
either did not know or ignored the matter. Despite
there being a counsel to help the king rule, none of
them had done anything either so it might have been
the king was ignoring the matter.*

*The death of King Kenneth appeared to be a
surprise to everyone, so he was sure it was a health
problem over a poisoning. He wondered what Princess
Isadora was going to do about those people. She has
appeared to not know anything about any of those*

people. King Kenneth did not share much with her as far as information to do with the kingdom and ruling. Sprague was pretty sure that was a foolish way to deal an heir to the throne, but no one had asked him and they were not likely to. No one had been much on it so far in his life, despite him seeing some mistakes other people were making. He would be willing to give advice if people asked.

Princess Isadora was given a chair just below her father's throne because she was not yet crowned and could not sit on the throne. Lord Sterling had come to stand beside her to provide her with information and advice. Then they waited for the guards to direct the people to her with their problems.

"I have started the plans for your coronation," Lord Sterling said.

"Thank you," Princess Isadora said, "Is there anything you need of me?"

"Not yet," Lord Sterling answered, "But I will let you know."

Princess Isadora nodded. Before they could talk about anything else, the first person stepped up and bowed. Princess Isadora did the same as her grandfather did and let the person gathered themselves before she prompted them to speak. Then she listened. This particular person was able to make their point in a succinct matter and not to waste any time. Princess Isadora appreciated that as she already knew some people could end up rambling with nervousness.

The issue was fairly easy to sort out as it was less of a puzzle and more of a decision by a higher authority. A guard would go back to the man's home with him and explain the solution to the neighbour, which seemed like it might go well since the man did not seem to be smug about the solution.

The next person stepped up and bowed. Princess Isadora did the same as she had before. She did notice Lord Sterling nodding his approval at how she was choosing to act and handle things. His responses made her feel proud of herself and more confident in her ability to deal with the court. Things went well for most of the morning. Then a man stepped forward and bowed, but there was an air of superiority surrounding him. There was a feeling in her gut told her that she should not trust the man. He was introduced as Gregory and the problem he was bringing before the court was a land dispute with his neighbour."

Prince Yester stopped. He was quiet for a moment and Valda glanced up at him. He yawned and blinked a few times.

"Perhaps it is time for bed," Valda said, "Perhaps we can continue tomorrow evening. I sent a note to Aldous about exchanging tales, so he will talk to you about that at lunch."

"Okay, thank you," Prince Yester said. He tried to cover another yawn.

"Take the lantern with you so you can find the correct room," Valda said.

"What about you?" Prince Yester asked.

"I have walked to my room in the dark multiple times," Valda said, "It is not difficult for me."

Prince Yester seemed to want to say something else, but he ended up yawning again. He got to his feet and picked up the lantern.

"Good night, Valda," Prince Yester said.

"Good night, Yester," Valda said with a smile. Prince Yester left the library. After a moment, Valda got to her feet and headed for her bedroom and her bed.

Valda made it to lunch to find out that Aldous and Prince Yester had gotten together briefly earlier to make plans. They had agreed to meet out in the garden after lunch to exchange tales. Valda ate as quickly as she could without drawing looks from others and left the dining room shortly after Aldous did. She had not seen Prince Yester, but there were too many people in the dining room or he may have had his meal sent to his suite.

Aldous got up one flight of stairs before he stopped and let Valda catch up to him.

"Coming to hear the stories?" Aldous asked.

"Of course," Valda answered, "I like to hear some of the stories you come up with and I really want to find out how good Yester is at telling stories."

"You like him," Aldous said.

"He is much better than any I have met so far," Valda replied, "Most of the princes who have shown up are stuck up and full of themselves. They also care nothing about books, poetry, or tales. I am not sure how people can care so little about knowledge."

"He seems to be a good sort," Aldous said.

"But he is the only child of his parents," Valda said, "Which would mean that I would have to move to the Island of Yester."

"That you will have to think about," Aldous said, "But I know you will make the best decision for you."

"Thank you," Valda said. They had reached the door out to the garden. Aldous went first and Valda followed him out. Prince Yester had not arrived yet. They went over to the area where there were multiple benches in a circle. They each sat down on their own bench and waited.

It was only five minutes later that the door opened and Prince Yester stepped out. He saw them and come over to them.

"I am sorry about being late," Prince Yester said, "I almost got lost trying to find the door to the castle garden."

"It is usually difficult to find the door the first time," Aldous said, "That is why I offered an escort as well as directions."

"I cannot believe that this castle has a garden," Prince Yester said.

"There is a chapel as well," Aldous said.

"Really?" Prince Yester asked.

"It is not used much," Valda answered.

"Well, I suppose we should get started," Prince Yester said, "Perhaps you should start."

"Very well," Aldous said, "This story is called The Man Broken By Love.

"For a hundred years the kingdom was ruled by a wicked queen. She had won eternal beauty and long life in a battle with one of the fairy folk. The kingdom had plenty of resources in which all its neighbours needed, so there should have been plenty of money for the people. However, the queen gathered it all and used it to indulge her pleasures. She used up the people in the same way. Many a young man was invited by several guards to come to the castle and was never seen again.

Fifty years into her reign, one of her head guards turned against her and started to plot against her. It took him twenty-five years to find others that were willing to join him. They searched for many years to find a way to kill the queen. Finally, they tracked down the creature who lost the battle. The fairy folk told them that the queen could only be killed by magic, but he was willing to help them. He gave them a scroll with a spell that would summon an assassin who would be willing to do the job for a price. They took the scroll and left the fairy folk alone.

They took the scroll back to the castle to read it. They found that the assassin was female and she took her price as the man who summoned her. The head guard tried it, but he was old and the spell would not work. The other man of the group was engaged to the handmaiden who was also in the group, but spoke about doing it himself. The cook, however, has a better idea. She suggests the queen's current lover, a man who the queen killed his love so he would be all hers. They knew he suffered in silence, but he suffers.

The head guard went to the man and offered him a chance to get rid of the queen through the spell that would take him as payment for the service. He accepted the scroll because he saw it as a way out of his situation and that then the queen would be dead. The head guard left him with the scroll. The queen was busy with something else and did not notice any of this.

The man, Valentin, barely waited for the door to close behind Cosmin, the head guard, before unrolling the scroll. The words glowed under his gaze as if begging for him to repeat them. He could not even see the rest of the spell, but Cosmin had told him how it worked and the price. Valentin didn't care about the price. The queen already claimed to own him, why not *have another woman saying the same thing? Others would be free to live their lives without starving. Valentin repeated the words exactly as they had been written.*

There was a puff of red smoke in front of him that slowly morphed into a woman. Her bottom half stayed as smoke as she looked around. She looked like the mythical genies that came out of lamps. Her red top barely covered her breasts while pushing them together and up. She had a red jewel in her navel, as well as gold hoop earrings, gold rings, and strands of gold string holding her black hair away from her face. The black eyes studied him as the red lips pressed together in a thoughtful frown.

"A man who is beaten down, but still with strength," her voice flowed like water over him as she moved around to study him from all angles.

Valentin stood still and waited for her to finish.

"A strange combination," she said, "And yet intriguing." She circled him a couple more times before stopping in front of him and letting the bottom half morph into legs covered in a long flowing skirt that matched her top. He noticed that she was barefoot.

"I am called Aislin," she said, "What are you called?"

"Valentin," he answered.

"I am pleased to meet you," Aislin said, "What is your wish, Valentin?"

"I wish for the queen to be killed," Valentin answered looking into her eyes, which were black but showed the pupil.

"And if I grant your wish?" Aislin asked.

"I understand what the price is," Valentin answered.

"You give freely," Aislin said, *"But do you have what you give?"*

"The woman I loved died as the hands of the queen," Valentin said, *"There is no one else that I love."*

"But the queen claims you," Aislin said, *"Under her laws, that makes you her property."*

"When she is dead, she will not own any property," Valentin said.

"I can grant your wish," Aislin said, *"But not in the way you want."*

"In what way then?" Valentin asked.

"You must destroy her," Aislin answered, *"I cannot get my price until she is dead and only you can do it."*

"How am I supposed to destroy her?" Valentin asked.

"This way," Ailsin answered. She disappeared into the puff of red smoke as did the scroll. When the smoke had cleared, there rested a curved dagger on the table. It was silver with a red tassel attached to the handle. Valentin lifted it and looked at it. The blade reflected Aislin instead of himself. Valentin understood what he had to do.

Valentin slipped into the queen's bed chamber which was the next room. He went to the bed and carefully slipped the dagger beside the bed, where it would be out of sight, but he could reach it while lying in bed. Then Valentin returned to his room to take a nap and be ready when the queen would call him.

The queen had fallen asleep and Valentin pretended to sleep. The guards had not quit shuffling outside the bed chamber. Slowly, the queen fell into a deeper sleep and the guard quieted down. Valentin waited half an hour longer before reaching for the dagger. His hand wrapped around the hilt as if it was waiting for him. He pulled it out and looked at it. In the dim light coming from the window, he could see Aislin's reflection in the blade. She smiled at him.

Valentin shut off all the thoughts starting to flood his brain and just let his arm doing what it wanted. The blade went into the queen's chest up to the hilt and then Valentin let go.

The queen's eyes opened and she screamed without making a sound. The dagger changed into a black version of Aislin. She threw her head back and gasped in ecstasy as the queen fought for life. The life and youth slowly drained out of the queen until she grew limp. Aislin reached a high pitch as she sucked the last of the queen's life away. Finally, the queen lay still. The black version changed to the full colour and rolled off the queen on to Valentin. Her lips hovered above him as her hand reached around to the back of his left shoulder.

"Now you are mine," Aislin whispered, "All for love."

A searing pain went from Aislin's hand on the back of his shoulder and into his skin. Valentin screamed out in pain until it got to be too much and he passed out.

Valentin woke the next morning in the healing house. He was on his stomach and his left shoulder hurt. He was feverish and the healer changed the bandage several times to avoid infection. When he recovered, the queen had been replaced by a kind king, who gave money back to the people and treated his *position as for the well-fare of the people. Valentin found the scar stayed a deep red, even after it had fully healed, and it was shaped like a circle with the silhouette of a full figured woman in the centre. He also found that he could not stay in the kingdom he had freed. Valentin put on a traveller's cloak and pack before going out to travel the world searching for his purpose.*

Valentin found it quickly as he travelled and fought battles that were all for love. He grew in strength, but the branding on his back kept him alone and broken. He was convinced he was doomed to never love again as he now belonged to Aislin. Valentin accepted this price for a kingdom's happiness and kept fighting for others to love. The end."

"That is a good story," Prince Yester said with a nod. It was a story Valda had heard before and she had enjoyed it again.

"Let us hear your tale," Aldous said.

"My story is titled Agatha and the egg," Prince Yester said, "*Once upon a time there lived a woman named Agatha. She was a kind woman and a loving woman. Agatha lived in a small village on the border between two kingdoms. At the age of eighteen, Agatha fell in love with a man who had come to the village and bought some farm land. Shortly after she married him and they settled down to farm.*

They were happy as farmers and over the years she produced two children with her husband; one boy and one girl. And they were happy together as a family. Their lives were simple and they needed nothing else in the world. Their children grew up healthy and the farm land never failed to produce enough to live on. Years passed in happy thought.

The children were half grown when a man stumbled into the village from across the border. He staggered as if drunk and spoke incoherently, but it was not alcohol that caused his issues. The man carried a disease no one in the village had seen in hundreds of years. And he passed it along to everyone who came near him.

The people of the village did not show signs of the disease immediately, but only after the man had died and been buried. Nothing the village healer could do stopped the disease from infecting the people. Soon most of the village had it. Agatha and her family were not immune as they had to go into the village for food and other supplies. Her husband was the first to get sick with her children not far behind him. Agatha herself did not get sick, but she was so busy taking care of her family to notice.

Most recovered from the plague the man had brought into the village, but many were placed in their new home of the village graveyard. Agatha's husband was placed there, but her children survived. Her joy of still having her children was barely able to overcome the loss of her husband. This joy did not last very long as she could not work the land herself and her children, although helpful, were too young. Agatha had no money to pay any man to come and work the land for her.

The village officials came out one and demanded Agatha sell the farm so it could be properly managed. They offered her a hut just outside the village and a small amount extra as payment for the farm. Agatha wanted to keep the farm, but she could see it was impossible for her to do so. With sadness in her heart and a tear in her eye, Agatha sold her farm and her home to the village officials. She packed up her children and the few personal belongings they had and moved to the two room hut the village officials had sold her.

Agatha did not know what to do about money aside from spend as little of it as possible to make it last longer. She had made a good wife, but none of those skills seemed to be needed by anyone else in the village. Agatha fed her children and cared for the small hut, but had little else she could do. The amount the village officials paid her was small and would keep them through the winter, but was not much more. Agatha also had what was left of the money she had shared with her husband, which would likely keep her and her children through the second winter. The rest of the village was still dealing with the after effects of the plague and could offer her nothing as they had no extra themselves.

Agatha did what she could to stretch the money thin while providing for her children. They lasted the third winter on what Agatha had grown in the small garden plot beside the hut. That winter her son turned ten and when spring came, he started doing jobs around the village to earn some money to help Agatha keep them fed. This ended when he was taken on as an apprentice. Agatha was paid a few coppers for her loss, but otherwise, she was left alone with her daughter.

The next winter Agatha's daughter managed to secure herself a position as maid in the household of one of the village officials. She sent Agatha a small part of her wages, but only until Agatha found out how *little she was making. Agatha did not want her daughter to give up a chance at a better life that her wages might offer, so she turned down the money. She had what she grew in her garden and a few coppers from the small amount she was able to sell since her children would not be there to help her eat them.*

And life stayed that way for Agatha for a couple years. She aged beyond her years and many times she wished she could live in the past when she was happy, but otherwise, she lived through each day.

It was late one winter night when there was a knock at Agatha's door. She opened it to find a man standing there. He wore a traveller's cloak and appeared to be near exhaustion. Behind him the snow fell heavily.

"Madam," the man said with a slight bow, "I have been turned away by many in this village. Will you grant me shelter to rest from my travels?"

"Yes," Agatha said, "Come in out of the weather and rest yourself."

The man stepped inside with relief and Agatha closed the door.

"I was just about to eat my supper," Agatha said gesturing toward the table, "It is not much, but you would like some?"

"Please," the man said, "If you can spare some."

"Sit," Agatha said before getting out another bowl. She dished up two bowls of the soup she had made. After setting them on the table, Agatha poured two cups of tea that she took to the table before sitting down.

The stranger had placed his pack down before taking the seat opposite her chair. He was about to pick up the spoon when she bowed her head. He did the same.

"Thank you for this food," Agatha spoke, "May it provide us warmth through this night. Amen."

Then they both raised their heads and started to eat. It was rather thin soup, but Agatha had little to put in it. The tea was weak, but Agatha did as she usually had to and added water to the tea leaves already in the pot. The stranger did not complain. He ate as if it was the greatest feast he had ever had.

When they had finished, Agatha gathered up the dishes and set them aside to wash when she was ready.

"The bed is this way," Agatha told the stranger, "Rest as long as you need." Agatha led the way into the bedroom. There was one bed and blankets on the floor where one of her children used to sleep.

"Thank you, Madam," the stranger said as he sank on to the bed. He took his boots off, but left the rest on before curling up under the blanket. Agatha gathered the bedding from the floor and went back out to the main room.

Agatha washed the dishes before making up the bedding near the fire pit. She blew out the candle before getting into bed. Agatha thanked God for the day and then went to sleep.

Agatha woke to the fire in embers and the wind no longer blowing outside the hut. She prayed for the day and then got out of bed. After washing up in the cold water she had set aside for that purpose, Agatha went to the window and opened one shutter to look out. The cold came in, but there was very little wind and the snow had stopped falling. Instead, there was a good amount on the ground, but not enough to stop people from going outside. Agatha closed the shutter and started preparing breakfast. She had the end of a loaf of bread and some cheese.

Agatha split them equally before pouring tea to go along with them. As she was finished those preparations, the stranger came from the bedroom. He had washed in the water she had left in the bedroom and put his boots back on.

"Good morning," Agatha greeted him as she gestured for him to sit at the table.

"Good morning," the stranger replied as he sat down in the chair. He waited until after she prayed over breakfast to start eating.

"It sounds like the storm has stopped," the stranger said.

"It has," Agatha replied, "There is a foot of snow on the ground and the sun is peeking out around the clouds."

"Then I shall be able to go on with my journey," the stranger said, "Thank you for helping me."

"You are welcome," Agatha replied.

They said nothing more until they had finished eating the food. Before Agatha could get to her feet, the stranger reached into his pocket and pulled out an egg. It was light blue with dark blue speckles.

"Please take this as a token of my gratitude," the stranger said. It was a beautiful egg, but there was no indication what type of creature was inside.

"Thank you," Agatha said as she accepted the egg. The stranger smiled before gathering his pack and leaving Agatha's hut. Agatha made a small nest out of a blanket and placed the egg in the middle of the table.

Then Agatha went about her day with her visitor being a distant memory by the end of the day.

The next afternoon there was another knock on the door. Agatha opened the door to find it was her neighbour, the wife of butcher and the village candle maker. She provided Agatha with candles and tea leaves through the winter in exchange for some potatoes in the fall.

"Come in," Agatha said.

"Good afternoon," the neighbour said as she entered Agatha's hut, "After that storm, I thought you could use some more tea leaves. I also brought a couple candles." The neighbour went and set her basket on the table. She saw the egg.

"What a beautiful egg," the neighbour said.

"Thank you," Agatha said, "A traveller stopped for rest and gave it to me."

"Would you think of selling it?" the neighbour asked, "I would give you a good price for it."

Agatha thought about it for several moments. She could use the money to provide for herself over the winter, but something about the egg made her not want to part with it.

"No, I do not think I will sell it," Agatha replied finally."

Prince Yester stopped the story because a loud voice came from the door into the castle as it opened. A large group of nobles and visiting princes stepped out of the castle and into the garden. Valda sighed loudly at the sight of them. She wished them gone, but there was nothing that could be done about them.

"I think we will have to continue the story another time," Aldous said.

"You are right," Prince Yester replied as he looked over his shoulder at the group. Some of the members had spotted them and headed over.

Valda was suddenly the centre of attention and questions and comments. Aldous in his usual manner slipped away. Valda did not see where Prince Yester went or even if he went anywhere. She was dragged along with the group as they toured the castle garden.

After trying much of the afternoon, Valda eventually found an opening and slipped away from the group. She went to her room for some peace and quiet before she had to go down for supper. Valda sat down with her notebook and got her quill ready. Then she started writing.

His voice does not ring, but sounds just like a king.
To listen to him sing, would make my heart spring.
But I am worried about the stick, should this not be the real thing.

Valda crossed out the paragraph and tried again.

His tale had no end, unlike my brother penned.
However, all my time I want to spend;
To see if he would be my friend.
If I offered my heart, would it he rend?
Would his heart be mine to tend?

Valda reread her words and once again crossed it out. Then she settled in her chair and stared out the window. She felt like she had emotions building up inside her that she could not find the words to express them and poetry did not help her this time. Or at least not writing it. Valda looked around and found one of the books of poetry she had borrowed from the library. She picked it up and started to flip through it. Only once she found the romantic section could she settle into her reading. That was the section she usually skipped when she read all poetry books. Valda read until she was called for supper.

After supper, Valda went to the library. This was the evening of the week when Aldous would not be there. No one else was there either. Valda sat down in the same chair she had sat in the night before. She did not have to wait long before the door to the library opened and Prince Yester stepped inside. He smiled at the sight of her and Valda felt her heart do a little flip. She smiled back.

Prince Yester sat down in the other chair.

"Ready to hear more?" Prince Yester asked.

"Yes," Valda answered as she settled in to listen to more of his beautiful voice.

"Princess Isadora noticed a brief movement from the back to the room. She looked and saw that it was Sprague. He was moving from one area of the room to another area. She was glad he was not leaving, but she was not sure why. Then she remembered what Medwin said about Sprague being a rogue. Maybe he could be of some use to her. She had wanted to be introduced to him since she saw him the graveyard at the funeral. But how to get there?

She realized the Gregory had not started explained the situation as she had not prompted him. There was some mumbling from the gallery. Lord Sterling tapped Princess Isadora on the arm. She realized she losing herself in thought and it came across strange to others.

"I am sorry," Princess Isadora said, "But I think it is time to end this session and finish with these matters another day. Court dismissed."

People bowed and then shuffled out.

"It is okay," Lord Sterling said, "It has been a long morning and understandable if you are tired. Will you be joining everyone else for lunch? Or would you rather rest and eat in your chambers?"

"I think I would prefer to eat in my chambers," Princess Isadora answered, "Thank you for understanding."

"Taking on such responsibility after burying your father so recently can be taxing," Lord Sterling said, "Take the time you need to rest and recuperate."

Princess Isadora nodded. Lord Sterling signalled to a couple guards, who escorted Princess Isadora to her chambers. She was worried about how to deal with things if the guards stayed outside her room, but she did not need to worry as they only escorted her to the door before leaving her. She went inside. There was no sign of anyone else having been there. Princess Isadora went to the window and opened it. She sat down on the sill and looked out but ignored anyone below in the garden. Though she was not sure how, but she would try and figure out how to get an introduction with Sprague after lunch.

Medwin sat down in the chair beside Sprague as he was waiting for lunch to be served. Sprague nodded to his friend, but did not start the conversation. His mind was on what happened in court that morning. He had been worried about Princess Isadora being far too much like her father, but she had been much better than he had thought. It was not until she did not immediately respond to that last case that he was concerned. However, she did not even listen to the case which was probably best.

"*It was a worry for a moment,*" *Medwin said,* "*But I would have thought her response should have been obvious to everyone in that room.*"

"*Your father figured she was tired,*" *Sprague said.*

"*She was alert right up until he stepped up to represent his case,*" *Medwin said.*

"*I am aware,*" *Sprague said,* "*And I can see the correct response the same as you. I think to find out why she did not just toss him on his ear, we would have to ask Princess Isadora.*"

"*I am not sure we will have access to her to ask,*" *Medwin said.*

"*We can try anyway,*" *Sprague said,* "*Because if she gives the dispute to the wrong side, it is going to be a problem. We owe it to her and the kingdom to warn her.*"

"*You think just anyone can go and talk to the queen-to-be?*" *Medwin asked.*

"*You remember the favour you owe me from yesterday?*" *Sprague asked,* "*Because I think the return favour might be talking to her.*"

"*I was hoping you would not use that,*" *Medwin answered,* "*But I guess I have no choice.*"

"*Well, you do,*" *Sprague said,* "*However, you might have trouble getting another favour out of me until the last one is repaid.*"

"*After lunch,*" *Medwin said.*

"*Shortly after,*" *Sprague said.*

"*Why?*" *Medwin asked.*

"*Because someone else might demand her attention first,*" *Sprague answered.*

"*My father announced that she will be resting this afternoon,*" *Medwin said.*

"And that stops what?" Sprague asked.
"All right," Medwin said, "Shortly after lunch."

Princess Isadora had just finished eating when there was a knock on the door to her chambers. She set the tray aside and got to her feet. When she opened the door and once again there was no one there. She looked down and saw another envelope. After picking it up, Princess Isadora closed the door. She took the envelope to her desk and opened it.

Isadora, Queen to be,

As you made no decision, I consider no agreement put in place. Due to this I am keeping the information and I will wait for you to make a decision regarding Gregory. If you are willing to rule in favour of Gregory, I will see it as you are in agreement with me and willing to work with me in exchange for the information.

You have until the next day court is held to make your decision. I hope you will make the right one.

Your Friend.

Princess Isadora wanted to deny Gregory the result, but once again she was conflicted because she wanted the information on her mother. This person was impatient if they were already sending her a letter to remind her about the offer. She had hoped the person would not destroy the information if there was not result in the matter brought before the court, which was the only good part of the letter. But she did not really need the letter, she would have assumed everything was the same until decisions were made in court.

There was a knock at Princess Isadora's chamber door. Princess Isadora did not immediately get up. She did not want to find another letter, unless it had the information about her mother which she very much doubted as she had not given the person anything. Then she thought about it and realized the person was not likely to send another letter until something happened. With a sigh, Princess Isadora got to her feet and went to the door. She opened it enough to peek out and saw it was Medwin standing in the hallway.

"I was wondering if you would be okay with a visitor," Medwin said.

Princess Isadora immediately felt like she was too tired to deal with anyone, but then she remembered she wanted Medwin to introduced her to Sprague. She had hoped Sprague could help her out the situation.

"Come in," Princess Isadora said as she opened the door enough for him to enter. Medwin stepped inside. Once she had closed the door, Princess Isadora led the way to the sitting area.

"How are you doing?" Medwin asked as they sat down.

"I wish my father was still alive," Princess Isadora answered, "He was supposed to teach me so much more than he did."

"You did well this morning in court," Medwin said.

"I appreciate your confidence in me," Princess Isadora said, "Nothing my father taught me helped. I was going back to my grandfather's lessons."

"At least you have some of the skills you need," Medwin said.

"Your father has offered to provide advice on any matter if I ask," Princess Isadora said, "Knowing I have access to more knowledge helps."

"There is a matter that I felt I should talk to you about," Medwin said, "I do not know if my father said

anything to you about it."

"What is it?" Princess Isadora asked.

"That last man who was about to present his case to the court," Medwin answered, "It was announced as a land dispute."

"What about the matter?" Princess Isadora asked, "I do not think I have heard anything about the matter before today."

"The land in dispute is along the kingdom's border," Medwin answered, "The landowner, who was at court this morning, does not have any land connecting to the border but he wants it to. This is the third time he had come to argue to get the land."

"Why does he want the land?" Princess Isadora asked.

"I do not know," Medwin answered, "He had brought his arguments but not the reason why. Your father denied him the request every time and I believe it was the best decision for the kingdom. With all your good decisions this morning, I was sure you would make the right decision, but someone else suggested I offer the advice to make sure you would continue to make good decisions.""

Prince Yester stopped at the end of the chapter. He might have gone on, but someone opened the door. Valda's maid stepped inside.

"I am coming," Valda said. Her maid bowed and then left the library.

"Unfortunately, tomorrow is when my father holds court," Valda told Prince Yester, "And I am supposed to be there, which means sleeping the night before."

"It is all right," Prince Yester said, "I understand. Go to sleep. We can continue reading tomorrow."

"Good night," Valda said with a smile before getting to her feet.

"Good night," Prince Yester responded with a smile.

DECISIONS ARE MADE AND PLANS COMMENCE

The week went by pleasantly for Valda. She spent plenty of time with Prince Yester and had gotten to the point of wanting to spend time with him over anyone else in the world. But certain worries crept into her mind also as she watched her father rule. At the end of the week, Valda wandered out and found Aldous in the library.

"What is your worry, my sister?" Aldous asked as Valda sat down in the other chair.

"I think I am in love," Valda said, "With Prince Yester."

"And why does that worry you?" Aldous asked, "He seems to be a wonderful person and definitely a good story teller. He told me one the other day about a white knight who turned into a grey knight after a journey at sea."

"I worry about what he is like at home," Valda said,

"What if he is charming here, but horrid in his own kingdom?"

"He does not seem false," Aldous said, "But yes, I know some of them are good at faking being good people. I cannot think of any other suggestion than travelling with him to his home to find out how he lives."

"It is a long journey," Valda said, "And few people leave once there."

"Did he not say something about his mother washing up on the shore and there had been a ship to take her home if she had wanted?" Aldous asked, "I think I remember him saying something about that. You take a guard, your maid, and a chaperone with you and you should be fine."

"I will have to get father's permission," Valda said.

"Tell him what you told me," Aldous said, "And he should have everything ready for your trip in less than a day."

"But whatever will you do with all those stranded princes?" Valda asked.

"Offer to show them out the back door," Aldous answered.

"That might cause a serious problem with the kingdoms neighbouring us," Valda said.

"Not really," Aldous said, "They are all second and third sons. No one will miss them."

"Father would not let you," Valda said.

"It depends on whether he has another run in with the group touring the castle," Aldous said.

"I suppose I should ask Yester if it is okay to travel back to his home with him," Valda said.

"Probably a good idea," Aldous said, "You do not

want talk to father and have him set everything up only to find out that Yester will not take you back home with him. Not that I think it will be a problem."

"But better to talk to him anyway," Valda said as she stood up.

"Good luck," Aldous said as she opened the library door. She nodded to him before she left and closed the door behind her.

Valda spent the afternoon avoiding the tour group and not able to find Prince Yester. It was likely he was hiding from the tour group as well. They were becoming a menace to everyone. It was only in the evening when they usually met up that, Valda finally saw him. He sat down in the usual chair across the small table from her.

"What is the Island of Yester like?" Valda asked before Yester could open the book.

"Compared to Proster, it is quiet," Prince Yester answered, "The ocean is a beautiful living thing. It provides everything we truly need, but we trade for things people want."

"I would like to see it," Valda said. Prince Yester looked surprised, but pleased.

"How does your father feel about you taking the trip?" Prince Yester asked.

"I have not gone to him for permission yet," Valda answered, "I did not want to ask him until I had asked you if it was okay."

"We can leave any time after your father gives his permission," Prince Yester said.

"I will ask him tomorrow," Valda said, "It will take a few days to get everything ready, but then we can leave."

"Sounds like a good plan," Prince Yester said.

"Until then we can keep going through the books," Valda said. Prince Yester smiled as he opened the book.

"*Medwin raised his eyebrow in a questioning matter.*

"*I would have thought seeing him and having the warning screaming in your head would have helped your decision," Medwin said.*

"*Because the situation is more complicated than that," Princess Isadora said.*

"*What do you mean?" Medwin asked.*

"*I got a letter yesterday with a powerful argument for ruling in favour of the man," Princess Isadora answered, "Despite it not being the best for the kingdom, it is making my decision harder."*

"*Does that mean you are going to rule in his favour?" Medwin asked. There was a large amount of concern in his voice.*

"*I have not made any decision," Princess Isadora answered, "It means I am still trying to make one."*

"*What argument did this letter give?" Medwin asked, "Because maybe we can figure out a reasonable way to help you make the decision that is best for the kingdom."*

"*They have information about my mother and are willing to give it to me in exchange for favours," Princess Isadora answered.*

Medwin opened his mouth to say something but then closed it as his mind went over what she had just said. Princess Isadora knew that he would have automatically gone with blocking all favours the person asked for because that was what was best for the kingdom. His response was that and only when he remembered how much she wanted to know about her mother did he rethink it. She was glad that he did not immediately suggest that she give up any chance to get the information about her mother.

"Did this person happen to tell you who they are?" Medwin asked.

"No," Princess Isadora answered, "And I have not been paying attention to people at court to figure out who it could be."

"Then we need to figure who it is and how to get the information without destroying the kingdom," Medwin said.

"I thought about it a little bit," Princess Isadora said, "But I do not really know where to start, but I thought maybe getting help would be a good idea."

"I can offer a little bit," Medwin said, "Mostly about the people in court. I have spent a lot of time in court and know the personalities. However, retrieving information from someone might be best if we ask for help from someone who has a skill set more effective to the matter."

"And who are you suggesting?" Princess Isadora asked.

"Sprague," Medwin answered, "That is his skill set."

"I would accept that," Princess Isadora said, "But I question whether we can trust him."

"Since he was the one who demanded I come and talk to you about the case, I would say we can trust him," Medwin said, "I think it best if we sort this out sooner than later because leaving until the next day of court would not be a good thing. I do not know why they want the land, but it cannot be a good thing to rule in their favour."

"Sounds like a good idea," Princess Isadora said, "When do you think is best to meet? I told people I would be resting for this afternoon, so I have some time today."

"I have to go find him," Medwin answered, "Then we can meet here. Hopefully, no one is watching you."

"They have something I want," Princess Isadora said, "What is the point of watching me?"

"To make sure you do not do anything against them," Medwin said, "Not to mention that you are queen-to-be, which puts you in added danger."

"I suppose there is that," Princess Isadora said, "Though I have not thought about it much."

"This kingdom is not known for attempts against the ruler," Medwin said.

"Not since the poisoning of my grandfather," Princess Isadora said.

"I forgot about that," Medwin said.

"It is easy to forget about that one because he survived it," Princess Isadora said, "I remember it because I spent my first while in the castle at his bedside. My father went off and found the antidote to save his life."

"Now I remember," Medwin said, "Plenty of people were worried that he would not return and at the time people were still expecting him to marry to provide more options for an heir."

"It took a long time for people to realize he would not be marrying and having more children," Princess Isadora said.

"The pressure to do the same will start to fall on

you," Medwin said.

"I am aware," Princess Isadora said, "But I have yet to decide what to do about it."

"My father has broadly hinted that we would be a good match," Medwin said, "But I keep trying to tell him our friendship is not that type of relationship. It is becoming a bit of a problem because he will not let me marry until you have shown a preference."

"I am sorry to hear that," Princess Isadora said, "I really do not have any idea what to do about marriage and providing an heir for the kingdom. I can talk to your father about the matter because there should be no reason why my indecision should stand in your way."

"I would appreciate that," Medwin said, "Normally, I would not ask such a thing of you but I am having trouble convincing him of anything myself."

"I will go talk to him tomorrow about it," Princess Isadora said.

"Thank you," Medwin said, "I should go find Sprague."

"Please," Princess Isadora said.

Medwin got up and left Princess Isadora's chambers. Princess Isadora did not move from her seat. She felt some relief now that she had talked to Medwin and they had a bit of a plan to deal with the situation. Some butterflies starting up in her stomach. Princess Isadora went through her thoughts to figure out what was causing them and realized it was the idea of meeting Sprague. She tried to shake that as it did not make sense.

In an attempt to deal with some of the nervous energy, Princess Isadora got up and went to the open *window in the other room. Standing there she looked out. Most of the court were out wandering in the garden; many of them in groups. She did not see Sprague or Medwin. Princess Isadora found herself twisting her fingers with the nervous energy and tried to hold them without movement.*

Princess Isadora did not know how long she was distracted when there was a knock on the door of her chambers. She went and opened it. Medwin was standing there with Sprague standing behind him. She held the door for them to enter before closing it.

"Princess Isadora, this is Sprague," Medwin said, "Sprague, this is Princess Isadora."

"A pleasure to meet you," Sprague said with a bow.

"You as well," Princess Isadora said before leading the way to the sitting area.

"We have a matter that we need to gain something someone else has," Princess Isadora said once they were settled, "But we do not know who that someone is."

"That makes it harder to acquire," Sprague said, "What do we know so far?"

"I was sent a letter from someone who is asking for favours," Princess Isadora answered, "Starting with ruling with the questionable side of the land dispute you asked Medwin to warn me about. In return for these favours, the person has offered information I want very badly. If I do not agree to do these favours, the person says they will destroy the information. The information is about my mother and my father was going to tell me eventually but he ran out time and no one else has the information."

"So, you want the information but you do not want

to do the favours?" Sprague asked.

"I want the information but not at the cost of the kingdom," Princess Isadora answered, "The letter suggested the ruling was not the full favour, but just the first of multiple favours they want."

"Do we have any ideas as to who the person who wrote this letter?" Sprague asked.

"There are a few people at court who would like to be the power behind the throne," Medwin answered, "But that is as far as we can narrow it down at the moment."

"It would be a start," Sprague said.

"Lord Hallam, Lady Gatlin, and Lord Stalvey," Medwin said, "There is a rumoured group but I do not know who is among them or whether they are real or not."

"I think I have heard those rumours as well," Sprague said, "But I have not heard or seen anything to suggest whether they are real. The other three might be best to start with."

"Lord Stalvey is very whiny and traditional," Princess Isadora said, "I cannot see him as being power hungry."

"Based on the way he made matches for his children, he is pushing for power," Medwin said, "He does try to appear anything but powerful in an effort to be underestimated. The other two are much more obvious in their intentions."

"We need to figure out who this is before the next day to hold court," Princess Isadora said, "That gives us a day and a half. Otherwise, I might have to rule in their favour to keep them from destroying the information and losing the chance to find out about my mother. It would be better to not have to do the favour and try to fix it later."

"We need to check the rooms of each of the three," Medwin said, "Though if they are keeping the information at their own houses, it will be much harder to find."

"There are three of us," Sprague said, "If each of us picks one of them, we can search the rooms today. Most of them are out in the garden for the afternoon and are unlikely to be there until they change for supper."

"If they are there, we will not be able to search the rooms until another time," Medwin said.

"Yes," Sprague said, "But we are on a limited time frame. It will only be if they are in the rooms that you will need me to sneak inside, so we should start by just searching."

"Okay," Princess Isadora said.

"People will be expecting you to be resting and not wandering the hallways," Medwin said.

"I will be fine," Princess Isadora said.

"Then we might as well go," Medwin said, "I will search Lord Hallam's rooms."

"I will search Lady Gatlin," Princess Isadora said, "We can meet back here."

They got up and left the room. Princess Isadora waited until the two men were out of sight before she slipped her ring on. Then she headed to Lady Gatlin's rooms.

It did not take long for Princess Isadora to arrive at Lady Gatlin's rooms. There were no guards outside and the door was not locked. The rooms were similar to Princess Isadora's chambers but the windows did not have as nice a view. No one was inside, so Princess

Isadora started searching. She tried to make it look like she had not been there.

Princess Isadora found some questionable items, but none of them had anything to do with the information she was looking for or the ruling of the land dispute. Also, nothing was enough of a threat to Princess Isadora and the kingdom. They may be a threat to some others, but Princess Isadora was sure they should be able to take care of themselves.

Princess Isadora was in the office area when she heard the door to the rooms open. There was laughter of two people. Princess Isadora moved as quietly as she could to where she could see the entry way. Lady Gatlin and Lord Vahn headed toward Lady Gatlin's bedroom as they made their intentions for the afternoon clear. Since Lord Vahn was known for his seduction of various ladies of the court, Princess Isadora was not surprised and doubted there was more to their relationship than their idea of a fun afternoon activity.

Once they had disappeared into the bedroom, Princess Isadora moved quickly and quietly toward the door to the rooms. She opened the door and slipped out before closing the door. She was glad that she had not taken off her ring. She headed back to her own chambers.

Medwin was hesitant as he moved towards Lord Hallam's rooms as he was careful about running into anyone who might ask him what he was doing. Most of the time people did not care, but occasionally people inquire if they saw him. So far he made it safely. There were no guards, which surprised Medwin as many of the nobles did have guards in their employment. But he was glad there was none. He tried the door and found it was not locked.

He opened the door enough to listen for anyone inside. When he did not hear any, Medwin stepped inside and closed the door behind him. He snuck into the office area. The desk was covered in papers and books and quills and dried inkpots. It looked like it had not been touched by a servant in years. To search the whole thing would take days. Medwin looked over the top layer without touching anything. Nothing stood out as being connected to Princess Isadora and her mother.

There was a paper about a village out near one of the borders and their fight with people from across the border. The villagers were not happy with the king and the fact that he refused to send members of the army to guard them. This could have been the connection to the land dispute. Medwin started reading instead of skimming the document. The names were wrong to be connected to the land dispute.

Noise from the other room caused Medwin to quit reading and freeze in place. Someone was moving around. It sounded like the person was heading to the office. Medwin looked around for some place to hide. There was a wardrobe. He pulled the door open and there was enough room for Medwin to squeeze in. He pulled the door closed behind him. Medwin heard the person entered the office area and sit down in the chair. It sounded like the person was settling in to work. Medwin wished for some way of getting out of the situation, but realized he was going to have to settle in for a long wait. He hoped nothing in the wardrobe would be needed today.

Sprague reached Lord Stalvey's rooms and tried the door. It was locked, but he did not let them stop him from getting inside. As he closed the door, Sprague stood and listened to see if anyone was in the rooms. Having heard no one, Sprague went to the office. The desk was fairly clean with only a pile of blank papers along with a quill and inkpot. Nothing there suggested any connection to Princess Isadora. Sprague started with the drawers. None of them were locked and none of them contained anything of interest.

Leaving the office area, Sprague moved to the bedroom. There was a bed, a dresser, and a wardrobe. Sprague started with the bed, but there was nothing hidden anywhere around the bed. He moved to the dresser. None of the drawers were locked and most of the stuff inside had to do with dressing Lord Stalvey. There was a box in the bottom drawer. Sprague took it out and opened it to see what was inside. It was filled with jewellery that definitely did not belong to Lord Stalvey as it was woman's jewellery. As much as it was tempting, Sprague put the box back in the drawer.

He moved on to the wardrobe. Most of the wardrobe was taken up with clothing and such items. There were boxes on the shelf, but nothing inside was what he was looking for, though there was an amulet he was tempted to relieve Lord Stalvey of it. He left it in the box and the box in the wardrobe. Sprague was just about to close the door when he noticed more room in the wardrobe than it looked from the inside. It did not take him long to open the false back. There was a pile of papers on a shelf. Sprague looked at the first page and it was something about a man named Alim and

Prince Kenneth. Sprague suspected that Prince Kenneth was a reference to King Kenneth and likely the rest of the papers were what he was looking for.

Sprague tucked the papers into his pocket before closing up the back of the wardrobe. He did the same to the wardrobe. Something was sending a warning to his gut to get out of there. Sprague headed for the door to the rooms. He slipped out and made sure the door was locked behind him. Then he headed around the corner. Once he was out of sight, Sprague could hear someone coming from the other direction at a fast pace. He was not sure where to hide, but then realized the person was stopping at Lord Stalvey's door. Sprague headed away from the rooms as quickly and quietly as he could."

Prince Yester stopped at the end of the chapter for several minutes, but it was still early in the evening and no reason to stop. He glanced at Valda and she nodded for him to continue with a smile.

"Princess Isadora arrived back at her chambers. No one else was there yet. She took off the ring and put it away before sitting down. Princess Isadora hoped the other two had better luck in their searches. She wondered how long it would take before they got back. Princess Isadora found herself unable to sit still, so she got to her feet and went to the window. She looked out. Not much had changed in the gardens and the people wandering around it.

There was a knock on the door of her chambers. She went and opened the door to find Sprague standing there. Princess Isadora let him in before closing the door behind him.

"Medwin has not returned yet," Princess Isadora

said as she led the way to the sitting area.

"Hopefully, he returns soon," Sprague said. They sat down.

"I did not come up with anything," Princess Isadora said, "Did you find anything?"

"I did," Sprague answered, "I think Lord Stalvey is someone who needs to be watched." He took some papers out of his pockets and offered them to Princess Isadora. She took them and started to skim the first page. Soon she was absorbed in her reading. The first page was about Alim and her father. Princess Isadora knew about Alim providing advice to her father and that Alim was from a far away land. He had been called home due to family issues and likely would not be back. The second page was about a thief named Marlene, who was hired by the court wizard and Prince Kenneth's cousin to steal something that could be used to poison the king.

The third page was about Prince Kenneth heading out to find the antidote to the poison. He took a thief to help him as well as some others. They kept coming across problems created by the wizard and cousin in their attempt to take over the kingdom and they fixed the issues. Prince Kenneth reached the dragon, who had the item he needed for the antidote, and abandoned the thief in the dragon's cave. Princess Isadora moved on to the fourth page and continued her reading. This page talked about the fact that the thief met Prince Kenneth months before the king was poisoned back when the wizard and the cousin hired her. When they met, they became lovers.

The thief was known as Mar when they met again, but Prince Kenneth did not recognize her as his lover.

Though he did find and recognized their daughter. Alim told Prince Kenneth to take Mar with him when he searched for the antidote as Mar knew where to find it because she was the one who brought the poison. She took him to it. It was in the dragon's possession. The dragon was willing to give the antidote to Prince Kenneth in exchange for the thief. Prince Kenneth having not recognized Mar as his lover willingly gave up the thief to the dragon. Only then did the dragon tell Prince Kenneth who Mar was. Then the dragon sent Prince Kenneth home with the antidote. As far as anyone knew Mar died in the dragon's cave.

Princess Isadora looked up from the papers. Sprague was sitting there waiting for her to finish.

"Did you read these?" Princess Isadora asked.

"No," Sprague answered, "I thought it best to bring them back here."

"According to these my mother was a thief," Princess Isadora said, "And she gave the enemy the poison they used on my grandfather."

"How are you feeling about getting this information?" Sprague asked.

"Conflicted," Princess Isadora answered, "According to these pages, she also helped retrieved the antidote. But her activities are far more understandable than his."

"What do you mean?" Sprague asked.

"She was hired to get the poison and then asked to help get the antidote," Princess Isadora answered, "But after travelling with her, my father never recognized her and then was willing to abandon her at the dragon's cave. Even if there was no connection between them, how could he leave her to the dragon?"

"I do not know," Sprague answered, "It does not make sense to me."

Princess Isadora put the pages down beside her and stared at them. Sprague left her to think the matter over. Several minutes went by before Princess Isadora looked up.

"If he did not find anything, what is taking Medwin so long?" Princess Isadora asked.

"I do not know, but hopefully he gets back soon," Sprague answered.

"Why do you steal things?" Princess Isadora asked.

"I started out because it was fun," Sprague answered, "And then I learned that stealing things can be valuable to people. It was a matter of making sure the right people were getting the items."

"Your father is a wizard," Princess Isadora said, "Why not get into magic?"

"Magic is a finicky thing," Sprague answered, "Not everyone can get the hang of it. I tried some when I was really young and it did not work for me. My brother was much better at it. Unfortunately, it meant my family has not known what to do with me since then. I started stealing things as a different sort of magic, which made things worse."

"So, they sent you here to figure it out?" Princess Isadora asked.

"My father needed help acquiring something and so he brought me here," Sprague answered, "I have found more to do here than there, so I stayed. Medwin has also found my skill set useful, among other people."

"Why would Medwin need your help?" Princess Isadora asked.

"His father is not allowing him to see the girl he

loves," Sprague answered.

"That was the girl you were with the other day," Princess Isadora said, "I saw you yesterday in the garden with her."

"Yes, that is Medwin's love," Sprague said.

"I told him I would speak to his father tomorrow on the matter," Princess Isadora said, "Because Lord Sterling hopes Medwin and I would get married, however, our relationship has never been that kind."

"You think it will change Lord Sterling's mind on the matter?" Sprague asked.

"It may not," Princess Isadora answered, "But I promised Medwin I would try. The biggest problem is that I have no romantic interest in my life at this moment."

"None?" Sprague asked. There was something in his voice Princess Isadora did not recognize, but it sent tingles through her body.

"Not so far," Princess Isadora answered. She felt like something caused a slight issue with her throat and she swallowed to try and get rid of it. There was some movement, but it was not gone. She almost wanted to find some water, however, she did not want to move from where she was sitting. Sprague did not seem to notice, but Princess Isadora was not sure whether he really did not notice or was pretending not to.

"Maybe Lord Sterling is worried about whether you will find someone," Sprague said, "After all, King Kenneth did not find anyone after your mother."

"I suppose that is a worry," Princess Isadora said, "But it is no reason to force unhappiness on someone else."

"If you do not want to cause anyone else to be

unhappy, what would make you happy?" Sprague asked.

"I do not know yet," Princess Isadora answered, "But based on what I know and how I feel on certain matters, I am looking for a more equal partnership than most marriages I have seen. Anyone who married me will end up being Queen consort and be under a lot of pressure from others to be called king. That is a lot to ask of someone."

"So, you need someone willing to accept that role," Sprague said.

"Most of the men I have met would not be willing to do that," Princess Isadora said, "They would rather take the role of king and control."

"You need to find someone smart and not power hungry," Sprague said.

"That is harder than you make it sound," Princess Isadora said.

"Have you searched very hard?" Sprague asked.

"I have," Princess Isadora answered, "I have not been successful in the matter so far. Medwin might fit the description but as we just mentioned he is not an option."

"Yes," Sprague said.

"I wonder where he is," Princess Isadora said, "He should be back by now."

Princess Isadora got to her feet. She took the papers into the office area. Princess Isadora put them under the false bottom of one of the drawers. Then she went back to the sitting area, where Sprague was still sitting. He got to his feet when he saw her and he stepped towards her. Princess Isadora turned to head for the door. She felt him behind her and could smell him. It made her want to stay there and soak him in, but she moved forward.

As if he could feel the same thing she did, Sprague took Princess Isadora's elbow and pulled her gently to face him. She found her hands resting against his chest and looking up at him. Sprague leaned down.

Medwin was finding his min mind wandering off as he leaned against the back of the wardrobe and stood in the darkness. He was trying to listen for movement outside the wardrobe, but it was hard to concentrate when the person was working quietly at their desk. He wondered if Princess Isadora or Sprague found the information. It would be good if they did as he was pretty sure he would not be able to do any more searching as his main focus was just getting out without getting caught.

There was a knock at the door to the rooms. The person working at the desk moved from it to answer the door. Medwin did not dare move as there was still a huge chance of him getting caught and there was nowhere else to hide. He could hear two voices and one he recognized as Sprague, but he did not hear the specific words. Then there was the sound of the door closing. Medwin did not know whether they were inside the rooms or outside. He was uncertain what to do when he heard the door open and close again. Someone came into the office area.

"Medwin?" Princess Isadora's voice came from outside the wardrobe. Medwin pushed open the door and stepped out. The light was really bright after being in the darkness for so long. Princess Isadora stood there and waited until he was ready. Medwin closed the

door behind him. He blinked a few times and then nodded that he was ready to go. They left the rooms without talking and headed back to Princess Isadora's chambers. When they reached them, they went inside and sat down.

"Sprague will be back in a few minutes," Princess Isadora said, "We were worried about you and thought you might have been caught."

"I almost was," Medwin said, "Lord Hallam was there when I went to search, but I did not realize it until I was already in the office. I did not find anything."

"Sprague found the information in Lord Stalvey's rooms," Princess Isadora said.

"So, we need to keep an eye on Lord Stalvey," Medwin said.

"We do," Princess Isadora said, "And figure out what to do about him because we do not know his plan."

"Well, if we have the information you do not have to worry about you having to do his favours," Medwin said, "That helps."

"It does," Princess Isadora said, "I just worry about what else he might try."

"We can think of something," Medwin said.

Lord Sterling was already in the throne room when Princess Isadora arrived the next morning. She sat down in the chair set up for her. The court would not start for several minutes.

"There are some matters that we need to discuss," Lord Sterling said.

"Medwin asked me to talk to you about something," Princess Isadora said, "But I assume the matters you *wish to discuss have to do with ruling the kingdom."*

"They do," Lord Sterling said, "And one of them has to do with a matter that will be brought before the court today."

"The man who did not get to present his case the other day?" Princess Isadora asked.

"Yes," Lord Sterling answered, "He brought his case before your father several times and King Kenneth refused him every time as providing him with access to the border will result in him bringing enemies across. We know this because he has been in prison for treason previously and he has spoken about his plans to others who told us."

"So, I should refuse him again," Princess Isadora said.

"If you want to rule this kingdom," Lord Sterling said.

"I planned on refusing him," Princess Isadora said, "Something about him makes me want to refuse him. I think he is working with a lord here at the castle."

"And who do you think he is working with?" Lord Sterling asked.

"Lord Stalvey," Princess Isadora answered, "Because Lord Stalvey tried to hold something over my head so I would rule in favour of this man."

"You said you were planning a ruling against him," Lord Sterling said.

"I did," Princess Isadora said, "I am not going to let someone else use me as a puppet."

"Good to know," Lord Sterling said, "Knowing that Lord Stalvey is behind it means we can keep an eye on him and his actions."

"Why did the man not stay in prison for treason?"

Princess Isadora asked.

"It was argued that he was unfairly punished for his actions," Lord Sterling answered, "Unfortunately, King Kenneth was willing to bend on the matter."

"Lord Stalvey was demanding to know when the council would meet next," Princess Isadora said.

"He was made a council member after Lord Afton had to go back to his estate due to a situation with his family," Lord Sterling said.

"I do not think it is a good idea for him to remain on the council," Princess Isadora said, "Send a letter to Lord Afton to see how his situation is doing and do not hold council until you can replace Lord Stalvey unless it is an emergency. If you can prove that this man has committed treason since he was released, put him back in."

"Yes, your Majesty," Lord Sterling said with a bow, "Anything else?"

"Medwin said he was in love and you are refusing to let him marry her," Princess Isadora answered, "I am not going to order you to do anything involving your son, but I am not going to marry him and break up his relationship."

Lord Sterling nodded without saying anything.

People started coming into the throne room. Princess Isadora waited until everyone was settled in before signalling things to start. The man, Gregory, stepped forward to present his case. He was confident that things would be ruled in his favour. Princess Isadora listened to him. His arguments were questionable and he was not likeable. When he was finally done, he waited for Princess Isadora to rule in his favour.

"*I have been told that my father refused you every time you have brought this to court before,*" Princess Isadora said.

Gregory nodded but his confidence was still present.

"*I have heard nothing to suggest he was wrong,*" Princess Isadora said, "*I deny your request.*"

"*You cannot,*" the man said as he was shocked at her words.

"*I can,*" Princess Isadora said, "*And if you try to bring this matter before this court again, you will be sent to prison.*"

The man stared in shock until one of the guards escorted him out. Princess Isadora glanced at Lord Stalvey without moving her head. A frown crossed his face and then he quickly switched back to blank expression. Court moved along to the next case."

Prince Yester stopped again. This time it was time to stop for the night. Prince Yester closed the book. He got to his feet.

"Good night," Valda said.

"Good night," Prince Yester replied. He left the library.

Valda knocked on the door to her father's office after lunch. She knew he was in there and that he was working.

"Come," her father's voice came through the door. Valda opened it and stepped inside. Her father put down his quill and looked up at her.

"What is it, my child?" King Waldemar asked.

"I want to go with Prince Yester to see his home," Valda answered, "I have fallen in love with him and wish to see his behaviour in his natural setting."

"And if he changes into someone whom you cannot love?" King Waldemar asked.

"Then I will return home," Valda answered, "And come back to my studies here."

"And if you find that he is whom you truly love?" King Waldemar asked.

"I will send a message for you to send my belongings," Valda answered, "And marry him."

"I have met the young prince from Yester," King Waldemar said, "And I approve the match if he is as you think he is. What would you have us do with the rest of the princes?"

"Aldous suggested sending them out the back door," Valda said. King Waldemar laughed.

"I appreciate his sense of humour," King Waldemar said, "Perhaps instead, we send you off without telling them and see how many will notice. There will be broad hints provided to them over a month. If at the end of the month, they have not left then I will consider the back door option."

"That should work," Valda smiled.

"In the meantime, there are plenty of things to get done for you to leave," King Waldemar said, "Starting with talking to the castle steward. If you see him in the hallway, let him know I want to talk to him."

"Yes, father," Valda said.

"And I will miss you," King Waldemar said.

"I will miss everything here," Valda said, "You, Aldous, and the library."

"I will see what I can find for books to send you every year," King Waldemar said, "Since I have been told the Island Kingdom of Yester lacks in that area."

"I would appreciate it," Valda said with a smile. She

left her father's office and closed the door.

Valda headed for her room. Her maid was tucking the clean sheets on to the bed.

"I need you to take a message to the prince of Yester," Valda said, "And to do so without gossiping or telling anyone what you are doing. Any word to anyone and you will find yourself without work and a bad reputation."

"Yes, My Lady," the maid said as she stopped what she was doing to pay attention to what Valda was saying.

"You will tell him that the king will arrange everything shortly," Valda said.

"Anything else?" the maid asked.

"No, that is all," Valda said, "Once you have finished delivering the message, come back as we have lots of packing to do."

"Yes, My Lady," the maid said.

"You will be packing your stuff as well," Valda said.

"Yes, my lady," the maid said.

"Go," Valda said. The maid bowed and then hurried off. Valda started packing for the trip. She was not sure quite what she would need as she had never been on any sort of trips, but she sorted everything into two piles; one to go with her now and the other to be sent once she was settled on the island of Yester. Valda found herself smiling for no reason other than she would be travelling with Prince Yester.

Two days later, Valda waited in her room for word that everyone was ready to leave. Her maid had taken her trunks and bags down to the carriage already. The guard she was being sent with would already be down there with his horse ready. She was not sure who was the chaperone, but she was getting impatient. Valda wanted to get going as the carriage was supposed to leave before dawn so no one or few people would know it was leaving.

There was a knock on the door.

"Come in," Valda called. The door opened and Lady Gildore stood there with a lantern in her hand. She was a widow, who took over some of the mothering duties to Valda after Valda's mother had died.

"Blow out the candle and come on," Lady Gildore said. Valda got to her feet quickly. She blew out the candle and followed Lady Gildore into the hallway. She closed the door before they headed down the hallway.

They did not meet anyone as they walked down through the castle to the front door. Outside in the court yard, everyone was waiting for them. Valda stopped to give her father a hug and kiss on the check. She hugged Aldous. Then she let herself be helped into the carriage. Lady Gildore was helped in after her. Then Prince Yester climbed in followed by his chaperone, who closed the door. The carriage started forward and they were finally off. Valda glanced out the window once before they left the court yard. There were no lights visible in any of the windows of the castle.

TRAVELLING OVER LAND AND SEA

There was little variation as they travelled across the kingdoms between Proster and the ocean. The days were a blur of landscape and the nights stopping at an inn along the road. Lady Gildore had brought her needle work to keep her occupied. Prince Yester's chaperone slept. Prince Yester spent the time reading tales out of a book he had to Valda. He had left the Thomas Merritt books back in Proster, but he had a book of tales he had brought with him.

Valda loved hearing the tales and would just sit and let his voice wash over her. Lady Gildore did not seem to mind the stories as she did her needle work. Then again Lady Gildore had read plenty of tales to Valda over the years, so it would not be much of a surprise she would enjoy hearing stories. It definitely helped pass the time.

It was more than a week from the time they left to when they arrived at the port city. They arrived in the evening, so they found a place to stay for the night. Valda was disappointed at their arrival in the port city because she had not been able to see the ocean due to the darkness. Prince Yester assured her that it would look better in the morning anyway.

Valda followed Lady Gildore out of the inn. Prince Yester and his chaperone had gone out earlier to get the carriage. The sun was coming into the city at a slant as if it was not quite decided to get up yet. Valda tried to think positive things, but the disappointment of not seeing the ocean last night was still too fresh in her mind.

"Come, my dear," Lady Gildore said, "No use pouting."

Valda looked around, but she could only see buildings and more buildings. There was no ocean in sight.

"We are going to see it so much over the next while that you will be tired of seeing it," Lady Gildore said.

"I suppose," Valda said without being soothed.

The carriage came up to them. It stopped and Prince Yester stepped out.

"Tell them to hurry," the voice of Prince Yester's chaperone said from inside the carriage.

"I am sorry about him," Prince Yester said, "He gets rude when he is impatient."

Prince Yester helped Valda and Lady Gildore into the carriage. Prince Yester's chaperone was frowning and his arms crossed over his chest. Prince Yester climbed inside the carriage and closed the door. The carriage started moving.

"The sooner we get back to Yester, the better," the

chaperone said.

"Why?" Valda asked.

"He just does not like travelling by ship," Prince Yester answered, "But there is no other way to get home."

"Traveling by ship is dangerous," the chaperone said, "You may think you are invincible because you are young, but do not be fooled. The ocean is not choosy about who it picks to pull below and drown. That is not even mentioning the kraken or the sirens or the leviathan or the sea dragons or the giant sharks. There are plenty of dangerous things out in that ocean ready to kill the unwary."

"There are plenty of wonders," Prince Yester said, "Not all of it trying to kill you. I mean how can everything that comes from there be so dangerous." Prince Yester gestured out the window. Valda looked out the window of the carriage and for the first time in her life she saw the ocean. She had read poetry about it, but now that she saw it for herself the poems did not do the sight justice.

The water was a greenish colour and not the blue she expected. There was movement like it truly was alive. She caught her breath and found herself unable to look away.

"It is beautiful, is it not?" Prince Yester asked.

Valda tried to answer him, but instead found herself just nodded. She wanted to touch it and smell it and see it from much closer. Then the view was cut off by another building. Valda looked at Prince Yester and he smiled at her as if he had had that reaction once.

"It is so beautiful," Valda said.

"You will not enjoy your first few days on it," the

chaperone said in a disgusted voice.

"Why did you come if you do not like travelling?" Lady Gildore asked the chaperone.

"Someone responsible had to come along," the chaperone answered.

Lady Gildore gave a snort as if she did not believe him to be either responsible or had to come. Valda hid a smile behind her hand and saw Prince Yester pressing his lips together to prevent his own smile.

"You will see the dangers when we board the ship," the chaperone said, "Just you wait."

No one spoke as they rode through the streets. Valda kept looking out the window in case she could get another view of the ocean, but it was always blocked by buildings. It disappointed her, but she was doing better than earlier because she had seen the ocean and it was as magical as she was expecting. She wanted to reach over and take Prince Yester's hand, but knew it would draw looks from his chaperone and Lady Gildore.

The carriage started down a hill and then slowly the ground flattened out. Then the carriage started a turn and Valda could see a bit of the ocean. She was hoping to see more, but the carriage came to a stop.

"We are at the dock," Prince Yester said. He opened the door and got out. Then he turned and helped Valda out. She looked around and saw not only the enchanting water of the ocean but the huge ship that was going to take them to Yester. It was so much bigger than Valda had thought after seeing ships in books. She felt so small standing on the dock looking up at it.

"Wow," Valda said.

"That is the Lady Tymeria," Prince Yester said, "She is one of the largest ships in the fleet."

"She is beautiful," Valda said.

"You will not feel that way when you are stuck on board," the chaperone said.

Valda ignored him. Prince Yester offered Valda his arm and she accepted it. He led the way to the gangplank, where he stopped.

"Permission to come on board," Prince Yester called.

"Granted," came the reply from the ship. They headed up the gangplank. It was a little tricky for Valda to keep her balance at first but Prince Yester was steady on his feet and kept her from falling. The ship itself rocked in the water. Valda looked around when they were standing on the deck. There was little luxury and more practicality to be seen. She did not mind that at all.

"Welcome on board, Young Master," a man said as he came up to them. He was well-muscled but short man. He was wearing clothing Valda has seen in books on sailing.

"And who are these fine guests?" the man asked.

"Captain Gagan, this is Princess Valda of Proster and her chaperone, Lady Gildore," Prince Yester said.

"Very nice to meet you both," Captain Gagan said with a bow, "I hope you enjoy your stay on my ship. I will have a man prepare your cabin and have your bags placed inside. We will be leaving on the evening tide, so you have plenty of time to get your sea legs before we leave dock."

"Thank you, Captain Gagan," Valda said, "Your ship is beautiful."

"She is," Captain Gagan said. He broke into a smile so wide it seemed almost too big for his face.

"I will give you the grand tour," Prince Yester said, "And we can leave Captain Gagan to his duties."

Captain Gagan nodded. Prince Yester took Valda toward a set of stairs to a higher deck. Lady Gildore followed.

It had been an interesting tour. Valda had read books on sailing but there was nothing like standing on an actual ship. It had taken her a short while before her legs no longer felt weak, but Prince Yester appeared to understand as he kept her arm in his for the tour. Now he was below talking to Captain Gagan about the journey. Valda was standing at the railing on the main deck and looking out over the sea.

The water glittered in the sunlight. It was far more blue up close than it had been from a distance. Occasionally there were ripples in the water, but she could not see what caused them. The movement of the water lapping at the side of the ship rocked it. It was a gentle movement and Valda found it to be relaxing.

The whole tour Prince Yester's chaperone kept warning about the first few days on the ocean along with getting caught in ropes that could drag a person under and storms that washed people overboard where they would drown. Valda was glad to get a break from the man when Captain Gagan announced the cabins were ready and he had gone down to make himself comfortable. Lady Gildore had gone down to the cabin she was going to be sharing with Valda to make sure all their bags made it from the inn and settle herself.

Valda wanted to reach down a put her hand in the water but it was much too far for her to reach. She could smell the salty air and something else. Valda could not identify the second smell and she had not asked Prince Yester about it yet. She would later when he was not so busy. He knew so much about the ship and its workings. Valda supposed that was expected of someone who lived on an island where the only way off was by ship. He hardly seemed the type to sit by and watch others work and more likely to volunteer to help and learn how to do those jobs with the people. It was part of why Valda loved him. Her parents had never been ones to let others do all the work when they could help. They especially liked to learn new skills from the people.

Learning was undervalued among those of the nobility as far as Valda was concerned. Too many of them acted like they knew everything, or if they did not know it the subject was beneath them. It frustrated Valda whenever she came up against it. She appreciated people who were willing to say they did not know anything on the subject and then be taught by someone else, no matter what station in society the other person was.

"What do you think so far?" Prince Yester's voice interrupted Valda's thoughts.

"It is wonderful," Valda answered turning to see him leaning against the railing next to her, "I have read so many books about the ocean, but nothing truly translates into seeing it for myself."

"I grew up in sight of the ocean and it still gives me that feeling," Prince Yester said, "It is just one of those awesome things of nature."

"What did your chaperone mean when he kept grumbling about things being not as pleasant once the ship is under way?" Valda asked.

"Many people get sea sick on ships," Prince Yester answered, "He certainly does. It usually goes away after the first week as it takes that long for the body to get used to being out on the water. Some people have it during the whole voyage."

"That does not sound good," Valda said.

"It is not," Prince Yester said, "And I have sympathy for anyone who gets it. The first time I stepped on to a ship I was sick for a couple days and I would not wish that on anyone. However, my chaperone always thinks people are mocking him when he is sick."

"That would be horrible," Valda said, "To mock someone who is sick."

"The sailors on this ship are meant to be the most experienced of those from Yester," Prince Yester said, "They usually are sympatric to those who suffer from sea sickness and I have never heard them make any comments about the chaperone. But he also thinks people in the court at home mock him, so it may just be his own mind."

"No one has told him that the world is not against him?" Valda asked.

"It does not work," Prince Yester answered, "He just thinks it is another way to mock him. It has been tried. I have gotten to the point where I ignore most of what he says, unless I asked him about a subject."

"How long until we get under way?" Valda asked.

"A few hours," Prince Yester answered, "We can sit in the pavilion on the upper deck to wait if you want."

"That sounds nice," Valda said.

Prince Yester led the way up the stairs to where the pavilion was set up with several chairs in the shade. It was all firmly attached to the deck of the ship so it did not move when the ship did or lost during a storm. Prince Yester sat down and Valda sat in the chair next to him.

"I never heard the end to the story about Agatha," Valda said, "You were interrupted by the group coming out of the castle and then I was not there when you and Aldous finished telling stories."

"I can finish it for you while we are waiting," Prince Yester said.

"Please," Valda said.

"Where did I have to stop?" Prince Yester asked.

"She had just turned down her neighbour's offer to buy the egg," Valda answered.

"Okay," Prince Yester said as he settled into his chair,

"Agatha's neighbour was disappointed but accepted Agatha's answer and went home without the egg. Agatha went about her day without thinking about the stranger, the egg, or her neighbour's request. The egg stayed on the table wrapped in the blanket, but otherwise, Agatha paid it no attention. She went about her life as usual.

The next week her neighbour visited again. The visit was fine until the neighbour went to leave, she saw the egg and asked again to buy it. Agatha once again turned her down. The neighbour left shortly after.

The winter was long and Agatha found herself struggling with the small amount of food in her cupboards. She started to trade for food stuff that others could spare. Agatha would do work for people. But for some reason she refused to sell or trade the egg. Her feeling about the egg was to keep it. Sometimes she wondered if it had been scrambled as the egg did not do anything. *It just sat there in the blanket and did not hatch. Maybe she was supposed to eat it, but she did not.*

The worst days were the ones Agatha was snowed in and could not offer her services to people as it meant she had to subsist on what little was left in her cupboards. She waited patiently for spring to arrive, but it was late. The cold and snow did not give up as if it was making up for something. Agatha survived day by day. She was melting snow and drinking it as her meals when she could not get food any other way. She had had hard winters before but this was the hardest during her lifetime and there were moments in what should have been the spring when she was not sure she would survive.

The first day of true spring, the sun shone down and the temperature warmed up. Agatha went out and enjoyed the day. She did jobs for others for food as the snow was not melted yet. Everyone was in a good mood as spring had arrived and that meant things would get better. In the evening, Agatha got back from helping others to find the last of the sun's rays were on the egg. It made the egg glow with a strange rainbow light. When the sun shifted off the egg, the glow was gone.

Agatha stared at the egg, but without the sun it was just an egg. It sat there in the blanket and did nothing as it had been since Agatha had been given it. With a shrug, Agatha got on to making supper with the food she had earned for the day. When she was done eating, Agatha went to bed.

Agatha found herself awake and looked around to see what woke her. There was moonlight coming in and lighting the room. She could not immediately see what disturbed her sleep. Agatha got out of bed to look around better. Nothing was amiss and nothing appeared different from earlier. Agatha was headed back to bed with the assumption that a dream woke her rather than noise. Then she heard it.

There was a loud cracking sound coming from the table. Agatha went to the table and looked down at the egg. There were two large cracks in it, but it was not yet open and she could not see what was inside. Agatha went a got a cup of water and brought it back to the table. She sat down and watched the egg. The movement of the egg was slow, but it was happening. There were a few moments where Agatha was worried that the creature inside would not survive, however, she remembered that if it could not get out on its own it would die anyway.

Movement inside caught Agatha's attention, something was tapping against the shell. The cracks got bigger. A small head peeked out. It appeared to be covered in fur rather than feathers. The creature got itself farther out of the shell. Not only did it have fur, but it looked more like a wild cat with a beak. Then Agatha noticed the wings on its back. The creature made a squeaking noise. Agatha offered it some water from the cup. It opened its beak and a tongue came out to lick up the water.

Agatha got up and got some of the softer leftovers from supper. She brought them back to the table and offered them to the creature. It ate everything provided.

"You are such a sweet thing," Agatha said as she petted the top of its head, "But what am I going to do with you? I can barely feed myself let alone something else."

The baby creature did not look up at the sound of her voice as its focus was the food. Agatha stopped petting it. The creature looked up and cherped. Agatha smiled at it and then went back to petting it.

"Such a sweet thing," Agatha said.

When the creature was finished eating and drinking, it curled up on the blanket away from the shell and settled into sleep. Agatha left it alone and watched it a moment. It started breathing evenly suggesting sleep. She smiled at it before going to her own bed and falling asleep.

The next morning Agatha woke to the sounds of the creature crying on the table. She got up and went over. It cherped happily at the sight of her. Agatha patted the creature and it snuggled into her hand.

"Such a sweet thing," Agatha said, "But what am I going to do with you?"

The creature cherped. It did not understand her, but she smiled at it and it seemed to smile back. Agatha left it long enough to refill the container of water. Then she got ready for the day. When Agatha was ready, she tucked the creature into her apron pocket because it cried when she tried to leave without it. It settled in without any further complaint.

Agatha worked as she usually did to get enough to feed herself, but also a little extra for the creature. The snow was melting and causing puddles, but nothing was growing yet. People offered her what they could, as they usually did. Agatha was able to get enough for herself and a little extra. The creature stayed in her pocket and was quiet.

At the end of the day, Agatha went home and ate

what she had been given for the day. She feed the creature before setting it in the blanket. It quickly fell asleep. Agatha smiled at it before going to bed herself.

A week passed the same way with Agatha working and the creature in her pocket. But as most babies do the creature grew bigger. The next week the creature stuck its head out to look around. People noticed the creature and Agatha was forced to explain how she got such a creature. One of the children was able to identify it as a griffon. Griffons were known for being loyal creatures, great hunters, and pure hearts.

The next week, the griffon was too big for Agatha's pocket and instead followed her around helping out with whatever he could. Agatha appreciated the help because the griffon was eating more and more as it grew. A few times the griffon wandered off and when he came back would be chewing on something. Since it did not make the griffon sick, Agatha did not worry about it. She heard from several people that they noticed fewer rodents around the village, which no one minded.

As the griffon got bigger, when he wandered off he would be gone longer and longer. Agatha did not mind as she knew he would always come back. The griffon started bringing back small animals for her to clean and cook. The griffon was not so interested in the animal once it was cooked, but he did not appear very hungry after his wanderings. This helped her a lot because she was still working on getting food from others. Agatha had planted her garden, but it would take a few weeks before she could harvest anything.

As the griffon got bigger, he became too big to share the house with Agatha because it was such a small house. One of the villagers, who was a carpenter, offered to make a shelter for the griffon. Agatha accepted, but worried about paying the man back, however, the villagers felt the griffon was its new mascot and thus the carpenter was willing to do the work for free.

Soon the griffon was big enough that Agatha was not worried about it when it disappeared. The griffon would bring back animals for Agatha to cook. She was occasionally able to give some to others. But she did not sell any of it when the griffon brought it to her as she felt it best to gift away what she did not need."

Prince Yester stopped telling the story. Valda looked around to see what caused him to stop.

"What happened?" Valda asked.

Before Prince Yester could answer, the ship lurched.

"We seem to be moving away from the docks," Prince Yester answered.

"I thought the ship would not be launching for hours," Valda said.

"So did I," Prince Yester said, "I will be right back once I have talked to the captain."

"Okay," Valda said.

Prince Yester got up and went off. Valda stayed seated. She felt restless being left behind, but it was best to wait as she was not used to her surroundings. It was still hard to wait.

Before Prince Yester came back, Lady Gildore came up the stairs and onto the deck. She looked around and then came over to Valda. Lady Gildore sat down in the chair.

"It would seem that we are leaving earlier than expected," Lady Gildore said.

"Prince Yester went off to see what is happening,"

Valda said.

"I see," Lady Gildore said, "What have you been doing?"

"I asked him to finish telling me a story he started telling me and Aldous back at the castle. He told me more but he still is not finished as he was interrupted by the movement of the ship."

"It is a good story?" Lady Gildore asked.

"So far," Valda answered, "I really want to hear the rest."

"Maybe you should suggest he write stories down," Lady Gildore said.

"Only if he seems really interested," Valda said, "I do not want him to feel like it would be an obligation when he would rather not do it at all."

Prince Yester came back up on deck and came over to them. He sat down in one of the other chairs.

"What did the captain say?" Valda asked.

"He is not sure what happened," Prince Yester answered, "It seems someone else was in a rush for us to get underway. The captain also said that sort of thing has been happening a lot recently and he just goes with it."

"Should be concerned about this?" Lady Gildore asked.

"I do not think so," Prince Yester answered, "Captain Cagan is superstitious, but otherwise a good captain. He will get us to Yester with as little problems as possible."

"It sounds like there will be some problems," Lady Gildore said.

"There is a section of ocean between here and there," Prince Yester said, "It is always stormy through there. Many ships have been sunk in their attempts to cross it, but Captain Cagan has crossed it more times than any other captain I know."

"Good to know," Lady Gildore said, "It is always good to have an expert around when going through dangerous situations."

"Have you been in many dangerous situations?" Prince Yester asked.

"I was not so proper in my youth," Lady Gildore answered, "It annoyed my family, but I managed to survive it all so I feel it was fine."

"Is that why you never married?" Valda asked.

"No," Lady Gildore answered, "I did not marry because the man who I loved was not available when I was."

"I am not sure I understand that statement," Prince Yester said, "You would be available any time after you turned eighteen."

"When I met him, I thought he was single," Lady Gildore said, "But it was him misinterpreting himself as he was looking for a mistress. I did not have any interest in being someone's mistress."

"What about now?" Prince Yester asked.

"I am long past being the subject of a man's interest," Lady Gildore answered.

"I have known plenty of people who find love late in life," Prince Yester said.

"I have known a few as well," Lady Gildore said, "But I have not been such a situation myself, so I do not look for it. If it happens, it happens, but I doubt it will."

Prince Yester looked almost like he would push his point, but then he decided not to do so. No one said anything else as the ship was now far enough from docks to start sailing.

"Should we go below?" Lady Gildore asked.

"No," Prince Yester answered, "If it is needed for us to below, we will be told."

"Good to know," Lady Gildore said.

"Right now we can just enjoy the voyage," Prince Yester said.

"That I can do easily," Lady Gildore said with a smile.

Valda enjoyed sailing as well. Neither she nor Lady Gildore got sick from the movement of the ship, however, Prince Yester's chaperone only came on deck when he had to and looked green. Prince Yester had no trouble with any of it. Valda, Lady Gildore, and Prince Yester sat on the deck. Occasionally Captain Cagan would sit with them and share stories from his life.

The captain had gotten his first job onboard a ship at ten and had only moved up from there. He had been born to a lady of the evening and chose life at sea because the ocean called him. Many who become ship captain are born into families with money and thus they can buy the men the position, but Captain Cagan worked his way up through the jobs on the ship. He had plenty of stories about the voyages he had taken, either when he was a sailor or as captain.

When Captain Cagan was busy, Prince Yester would be the one telling stories. He did not finish the story about Agatha and the Egg because Lady Gildore had not heard the first part and he did not really want to start in the middle with her listening. As much as she wanted to hear the end of it, Valda accepted listening to other stories as Prince Yester seemed to have an endless amount to tell.

There were times when Prince Yester helped out the crew and during those times Valda and Lady Gildore would just talk. It made for pleasant time for the first week. They continued to do that for the second week, but they were interrupted by the chaperone feeling well enough to join them on deck. He still did not look well, but he was doing better. The big problem was that he was not interested in hearing stories or listening quietly to the conversation. Instead, he sat and complained, which just annoyed everyone else. Unfortunately, when on a ship there were not much as far as places to hide from others. The captain would find stuff for the chaperone to do, but that only helped a little.

Early evening a few weeks into the journey found Valda and Prince Yester on deck trying to avoid the chaperone's complaints and just enjoying the weather. It was warm with a slight wind. For a change Valda has been telling Prince Yester one of the stories her brother, Aldous, had told her. They were both having fun when suddenly something caused the ship to move to one side.

"What is that?" Valda asked as she clutched the arms of her chair.

"We must be entering the dangerous section," Prince Yester answered, "We should probably get below before the storms hit."

"Okay," Valda said. She got to her feet as the ship shifted again and only the fact that she was still holding on to the chair saved her from sliding across the deck.

"We need to be careful," Prince Yester said as he helped her back into the chair. Valda nodded. They held hands as the ship started rocking and the wind whipped up to make things even harder. Before they could reach the stairs, a wave came up and washed over the ship. Prince Yester tightened his grip on Valda and braced himself as the water hit them. Unfortunately, it was not enough and the water knocked them down. It pulled them over the railing and into the ocean.

Prince Yester tried to keep himself from being dragged under while holding on to Valda, who had grabbed his arm with her other hand. She also fought to keep her own head above water. Valda felt water in her lungs but she could not cough immediately because her head was under water. When she managed to get into the air, Valda coughed up the water but more seemed to get in.

Valda felt her vision going grey as she struggled to keep her hold on Prince Yester. He grabbed her with his other hand and tried to pull her to the surface with him. Valda kicked upwards, but she was not sure her legs were working anymore. Her head came out of the water enough for her to spit out some water and get some air. It caused the greyness to fade a little, but her body felt like it was out of energy to keep going. Valda tried to look around for the ship. The sky had darkened and it was impossible to see anything above the waves.

Valda felt her hands slip and she lost her hold on Prince Yester. Her head dipped under. Prince Yester pulled her up, but she did not manage to break the surface of the water. He tried again, however, she just dragged him down as much as she was fighting not to. Valda's vision was once again fading to grey. Not only was she sinking in the water, but she felt herself sinking into darkness in her own head. She completely lost her grip on Prince Yester and could feel he was letting go of her. As she was in the last of her conscious, Valda felt someone grab her under the arms. But before she could really form that thought the blackness was all encompassing.

LOST AT SEA

Valda felt the water lapping at her feet as she regained consciousness. The sand beneath her was soft, but the stuff in her mouth felt gritty. She remembered the storm and being washed overboard. There were even memories of struggling for air. As she had given in there had been someone else in the water with her. Valda had wondered who it had been and why.

Deciding to figure out why, Valda sat up and opened her eyes. She was sitting under a tree on the beach of a tiny island. There were a handful of trees between edges of what would otherwise be a pile of sand. Lying next to Valda was Prince Yester and he had not woken up yet.

Valda looked around for anyone else from the ship, but did not see anyone or any debris. The ship must have survived the storm with most of the crew onboard, just some minor guests lost. Captain Cagan probably had not noticed until the storm was over since they should have been below.

Prince Yester woke with a cough and exhaling some of the water. He sat up and coughed until it was gone before lying back down.

"Are we still alive?" he asked as he closed his eyes.

"As far as I know," Valda answered, "But unless rescue is soon we may die of dehydration and starvation as there is nothing but trees on this island."

"How many trees?" Prince Yester asked. Valda counted them.

"Seven," Valda answered.

"Are you sure?" Prince Yester asked.

"Including the one we are lying under," Valda answered, "Why does it matter?"

"There are legends attached to certain islands," Prince Yester answered, "And the main difference between the islands is the number of trees."

"What is the legend of the island with seven trees?" Valda asked.

"I am trying to remember," Prince Yester answered, "I know one through four and eight to thirteen, but I cannot remember seven."

Valda did not say anything hoping he could use the quiet to remember, it could save their lives. She looked around, but there was little else to see. The waves of salt water continued to lap at her feet because she had not moved them. Prince Yester's boots had been pulled up out of the water. Valda noticed that her slippers were missing, but given everything else going on that did not seem to be a big matter; they would make walking on the sand harder. Prince Yester was muttering to himself and Valda barely caught what he was saying.

"The Grey Knight," Prince Yester said, "The

Stranded Sailor, The Petty Pirate, Dragon Tears, and then." Prince Yester was silent as he tried to remember. After a long period of silence from him, Prince Yester opened his eyes and slowly sat up.

"I cannot remember five to seven," Prince Yester said, "And I should remember six because that was my mother's favourite one."

"Why was it her favourite?" Valda asked.

"She liked the characters or something like that," Prince Yester answered, "It has been far too long since I heard it."

"Do the stories connect?" Valda asked, "Would telling one help you remember the others?"

"They are not connected in any way, except they all talk about something that happened on the islands," Prince Yester answered, "But telling one might help me remember the others."

"How did a dragon end up on one of these islands?" Valda asked.

"It was not a dragon exactly," Prince Yester answered, "But the tear of a dragon."

"Is there something special about dragon tears?" Valda asked, "I have never heard of them being mentioned specifically in all the stories I have read."

"Depending on what kind of dragon, it will shed tears which become jewels," Prince Yester answered, "Most people I tell do not believe this, but one of the jewels in the crown of Yester is a dragon's tear."

"I would believe that," Valda said.

"Really?" Prince Yester asked, "Most people I tell that to do not believe in dragons."

"An advisor to the throne Proster a couple generations back owned a dragon," Valda said, "It is resting on her shoulder in her portrait."

"Wow," Prince Yester said, "None that I have seen in books or heard of were small enough to sit on a person's shoulder except when they were babies."

"It must have been a miniature dragon," Valda said, "Because I have not seen or heard of one that small either, but the portrait shows a dragon and the story is that she had a dragon as a pet."

"That must have been something to see," Prince Yester said, "What happened to the dragon when she died?"

"I do not know," Valda answered, "I do not remember hearing about her death or what happened. It might have been something my parents did not feel I needed to know and then when I was old enough I did not look it up for myself. But me telling you about her is not going to help you remember the stories. What does a dragon's tear look like?"

"It is about the size of an adult knuckle and it looks like a diamond except there is a tint of white to it," Prince Yester answered, "It is tear shaped as if cut that way. It is prized most by pirates and wizards. The pirates believe it brings them luck and the wizards use it in the spells."

"So, how did one end up on an island?" Valda asked.

"Long time ago," Prince Yester said,

"There was a nobleman's daughter who had been sent to another kingdom as a messenger. She had done what her father asked, but the man she was promised to take her in and marry her was not in the condition promised, so she returned on the ship to Yester. Before she left, the king had given her a box as compensation for having to leave rather than marry. She accepted the

box and boarded the ship.

While the captain may have been happy to have a passenger on the return trip, the nobleman's daughter was not happy about returning. She liked her family and Yester just fine, but she had hoped to marry while she was young and still considered eligible. Her fear came from a maiden aunt she had who was always sniping at people and spent her time gossiping because she had nothing better to do.

After making sure her baggage was in her cabin, the nobleman's daughter stood at the railing staring out at the ocean. She ignored the land behind her as if the ship had already left it behind. The crew got the ship ready while she did. The captain was busy and as such left her alone with her thoughts and worries. If he had the time, he would stop to talk to her as he had spent plenty of time talking to her on the journey to bring her to this kingdom and found her an interesting conversationalist. Had there been less social issues he probably would have asked for her hand in marriage as he was young and unmarried and interested in her. Whether she had noticed his attentions, or not, she never revealed, though she seemed to enjoy talking to him.

When the ship was ready, it set sail. The nobleman's daughter breathed in the sea air and continued to stare out at the ocean. Her mind must have been busy turning over things in her mind. It must have been a lot for her to ponder as she did not move much despite rain starting. The cold water did nothing to make her move. Some sailors glanced at her in worry because most passengers would have gone below at the first drop of water. The sailors themselves being so used to the water they barely noticed the soaking.

The nobleman's daughter was much more wet than dry by the time the captain noticed she was standing by the railing in the rain. He went over and encouraged her to go below. At first she did not move, but eventually, he was able to convince her. He took her to her cabin where he wrapped her in a blanket to warm her up. He sat there until she agreed to change into dry clothes and only then did he step out. When she was finished changing, the captain took her to the dining area and sat with her to talk. The captain had the cook provide both of them with a cup of grog, but he drank his much more slowly. She felt the alcohol warm her up.

They sat and talked over everything that had happened. Since the captain had not left his ship, he was not aware of all that had occurred while she was visiting the kingdom. She told him about the man who she had supposed to marry and the horror of her finding out about him, The nobleman's daughter held herself to an expressionless face and voice, but the captain could see the pain radiating from her eyes. His instinct to wrap his arms around her and comfort her was stopped by the fact that they were sitting in a public place on the ship. He hardly wanted to be accused of molesting a nobleman's daughter who was well above his station.

Only when his crew needed him, did the captain leave the nobleman's daughter alone and then only briefly. At first she was ambivalent to his presence and she could have been talking to anyone, but as the alcohol started to work she began to look at him with appreciation. When she finished her tale of woe, she *asked how his time on land went. He was honest about his time as it was mostly repairs and upkeep on the ship. His crew may have taken in the sights and the comforts of the town. Captain did not admit he had turned down the comforts of the town because the nobleman's daughter was far too much on his mind as he worried she may feel uncomfortable around him over such admissions.*

The nobleman's daughter found her mood much improved after warming up and having the drink of grog. When the captain got up to get another drink for them, she asked that he not get her more alcohol. He explained that everyone on board was provided with one drink of grog a day and no more, so he could not get more for them. Instead, he came back with water. For the first time since she boarded, the nobleman's daughter found herself interested in life on board ship. The captain found warmth flow through him at her interest and was more than willing to tell her about it, though he was careful to watch for any sign of boredom from her. She did not show any signs of it, so he kept talking. His voice made her feel good and safe so the nobleman's daughter listened to everything he had to say.

The first week of the voyage was calm and the captain was able to spend time with the nobleman's daughter. They would sit and talk for hours. The captain felt his emotions towards her get bigger and whenever they had to part it caused him great sadness. He would try to suppress those thoughts as he knew they were inappropriate for a man lower than her socially. His first mate reminded him plenty that such a match would never be approved by her family.

The nobleman's daughter was also feeling the emotions she should not have towards someone who was not of her social status. She knew her father would not want her to marry a ship captain. It was not that her family were against ship captains as it was a respected occupation, however, if they were not of noble upbringing that was the problem. This captain was not of a noble family. But she could not help her feelings towards the captain.

The second week the weather turned dark and it rained with limited breaks from it. The captain found himself needed much more by the crew. The conversations between the captain and the nobleman's daughter became less frequent. At first she would sit somewhere they would usually talk if he had time, but as the week wore on she would sit in her cabin and read. She did not try to spend time on deck as it would distract the captain in his attempts to get her to stay dry.

As she sat in her cabin reading, the nobleman's daughter noticed the box the king had given her as an apology for her non-marriage. She had never looked inside as the pain from the experience had caused her to not be interested in it. But now it piqued her interest. Not so much for keeping the gift but to know what it was. Finally, she gathered the box and opened it. In the box were jewels of all sorts. None in settings, all of them were loose in the box. They were cut beautifully. It was probably more jewels than her king had in his crown.

The nobleman's daughter was forced to wonder why such a large gift for such an experience. Was it the length she went to get there? Was it the potential bad experience with the possible groom? Was it the embarrassment of the whole situation? The king probably meant the gift to appease the nobleman's daughter, but instead, it made her upset. She closed the box and put it somewhere she could not see it. She was not sure what she would do with it yet, but she would figure it out later. Maybe when she had calmed down or did not feel so emotional about the whole experience.

Instead, she left her cabin and went to the dining area, however, there was nothing to keep her there. She left and began to wander the ship. The sailors she met greeted her and otherwise left her alone. The nobleman's daughter came upon the captain as he was stepping out of his own cabin. He greeted her. So much emotion welled up inside her at the sight of him and overwhelmed her. It surprised both of them when she wrapped her arms around him and pressed her lips to his.

It was the third week into the voyage and the weather had not gotten better. Things between the nobleman's daughter and the captain had been turned into something frowned on by society, but neither would worry about the consequences just yet. It would still be another couple of weeks before society would judge them on the matter. The crew of the ship said nothing to either of them, even though it was quite obvious to the crew what was going on.

One day the nobleman's daughter was left alone because of the storm that was coming and she had spent some time in her cabin. She was going through her bags and came across the box of jewels from the king. The anger towards the king has lessened in her mind, but she still did not want to keep the jewels. Many people would have found other uses for the jewels, especially if they were in a relationship not sanctioned by society. However, the nobleman's daughter had never needed anything in her life and such thoughts do not occur to her. Her idea was to get rid of the jewels and the easiest way to do so while at sea was to throw it overboard.

Gathering the box, the nobleman's daughter left her cabin and headed for the deck. No one stopped her as she went up, but they probably should have as the stormy waters were rocking ship. But she made it as far the railing without a problem and without being seen by the captain, who would have sent her back below. Without ceremony she opened the box and dumped the jewels into the water. Once they were gone, she closed the box and then turned to go back below.

The ship went sharply to one side and she fell against the railing. The nobleman's daughter grabbed the railing and held on tight as the ship shifted further to the side and she had to grip the wood tighter to avoid going over the side. She heard her name being called but there was nothing she could do. The waves came up over the side of the ship and washed over her before the ship could right itself. The nobleman's daughter tried to stay where she was but the water was too much and it dragged her overboard.

The nobleman's daughter managed to fight her way to the surface of the water and looked around. The wave had taken her a distance from the ship. She could hear the captain calling her. The nobleman's daughter *fought to get back to the ship, but the wave kept pulling her away from it. She could not see what the captain was doing as water kept getting in her eyes and she was left swimming in the direction of the dots of light she hoped were lanterns on the ship.*

The waves dragged her farther and farther away from the ship. She fought for a long time in her attempt to swim back to the ship until she felt like she ran out of strength. Then she did everything she could to keep her head above the water. The dots of light got farther away from her, though she was sure the captain would be trying to save her. The storm was making sure it was impossible for the two to reach each other.

The nobleman's daughter felt foolish for going on deck in a storm because she knew better. The captain had told her what would happen. But she was still so focused on her emotional response to the jewels rather than on the practical aspects of getting rid of them. She had done much in her life based on her emotions and not on practicality. There had been consequences before but never to this extent. The only choice in life she was happy with at this moment was learning to swim, which her father had frowned on at the time. But she had not let his concerns stop her from learning how to swim.

Her muscles stopped working as exhaustion overcame the nobleman's daughter. She took a deep breath before her head slid below the surface of the water. As she started to choke on the air and her body was demanding more, she saw something in the water in front of her. The nobleman's daughter could feel herself losing consciousness, but fought it. Whatever was in the water with her was human shaped from the top up and a fish from the bottom down. It grabbed her and pulled her up to the surface before she passed out. She managed to gasp in air and it brought her back. She coughed.

Whatever was holding her did not let her go, which was good because she could not have held her head out of the water. But the being did not stay still in the water and instead started swimming with the nobleman's daughter. After a few minutes, the exhaustion was too much and she could feel herself falling asleep despite being dragged through the rough waves. Somehow she fell asleep.

The nobleman's daughter woke up lying on a beach. She looked around found herself on a small island with four trees and nothing else. There were drag marks in the sand, which appeared to be marks left by a fishtail. She got up and wandered the island. There was nothing other than the trees and walking all the way around did not take long. Based on where the sun was in the sky, it was mid-morning. The nobleman's daughter sat down under one of the trees as she was not sure what else to do.

She had tilted her head and was staring out at the ocean when she noticed something shiny in the sand. Curious about it, she got up and went over to where the shiny object was. Bending down, she picked it up. The shiny object was a dragon's tear. She wondered if it was one of the jewels from the box she had dumped into the water. If it had been, she wondered how the king had gotten a dragon's tear. They were very rare and difficult to obtain.

The nobleman's daughter sat back down under the

tree and held the dragon's tear in her hand. If it had washed up, why had only this one arrived and not any of the rest of the jewels done so as well? Because none of them were in the sand along with the dragon's tear. Not that she wanted to see any of them again. She sat there and studied the dragon's tear. It was a perfect shaped tear with that cloudy centre and likely worth a lot of money.

The sun shined between the branches of the tree and directly onto the dragon's tear. The light reflected from the tear and out into the ocean. The nobleman's daughter held out her hand to keep the dragon's tear in the sunlight. She was not sure why, but felt that she needed to do it. As the sun moved, she moved the dragon's tear to stay in the light while still reflecting out at the same spot.

When the sunset, the nobleman's daughter curled up in a ball and fell asleep with the dragon's tear clutched in her hand. There was nothing to eat, but so much had happened and she was tired so more than able to sleep with an empty stomach. Thirst was a bigger problem, however, it did not stop her. At some point during the night, she was sure she had woken up and saw mermaids frolicking in the moonlight. But she was not so sure it had been real.

The next day, the nobleman's daughter did the same as the day before. She was hungry and thirsty, but there was nothing to eat or drink on the island. The trees did not produce any fruit, just branches with leaves. The leaves did not seem to be any kind of edible. She was not sure what to do, so she sat there holding the dragon's tear.

Slightly after the sun hit its height in the sky, the

nobleman's daughter saw a dark spot on the horizon. She tried not to be excited as it could have been anything. As it got closer, she could see that it was a ship. However, she could not see anything specific about the ship. She kept the dragon's tear in the light and reflected out towards the ship. When the ship was close enough that she could see more details, she finally closed her hand. She put the dragon's tear in her pocket. She no longer wanted to get rid of the dragon's tear, even if she did not want to see the rest of the jewels again.

The ship was the one captained by her lover and he was one of those who arrived on the island in the long boat. She was more than willing to be swept up in his arms when he stepped on to the sand of the island. He had brought a water skin and she was able to get a drink before she joined him in the long boat to be taken back to the ship. They did not speak until they were back at the ship and sitting in the dining room so she could eat something.

He had seen her go overboard and almost went after her, but his crew stopped him. His first mate convinced him that it would be better to keep searching for the nobleman's daughter when the storm is over. That was what they did. The captain had been worried they would not find her when he saw the reflected light and followed it to the island. She showed him the dragon's tear and explained about the box of jewels, including apologizing for not thinking it through and going on deck in a storm. He forgave her as long as she promised not to do it again and she did.

Since they were now passed the area known for storms, the rest of the voyage was calm and quiet. The nobleman's daughter and the captain continued their relationship, but now concerns were becoming more than wisps of thoughts. They ignored them though. The crew said nothing, even the first mate was silent on the matter. Perhaps it was that they could see both were happy and knew it would be hard enough when they reached land.

Reaching land, the nobleman arrived to whisk his daughter away. She did not really want to go but there was no choice. Her father had spent the time since he had heard about her return trying to set up another marriage for her. He had not formalized one, but there were plans. There was nothing she could do about his plans as he had no interest in her opinion on the matter. She said nothing about her happiness with the captain because her father would have accused the captain of assault.

The nobleman's daughter did not see or hear from the captain from the time her father took her away. She did not know if he was still in the kingdom or had been sent off again. Then just as her father was trying to formalize the marriage details, they received a summons by the king. The nobleman and his daughter were both listed in the summons, so they went. When they arrived, the captain was there waiting with the king.

The king explained that the captain was asking for the daughter's hand in marriage. The nobleman did not want to grant such a request as the captain was not of noble birth. The fact that the captain had earned his position and everything he had did not matter to the nobleman. However, the king saw the captain's hard work as worth the hand of the nobleman's daughter.

The king overruled the nobleman and decided to give the daughter to the captain for marriage and the nobleman would pay for the wedding in consequence for his objection to the matter.

The daughter was so happy as she got to marry the man she loved. In thanks to the king, she gave him the dragon's tear. The king accepted the jewel with a warm smile and she understood that he arranged everything because he believed in love. It felt good to give the king the dragon's tear as she knew he deserved it and she no longer needed it. She had something she wanted more."

Prince Yester stopped and Valda smiled. She liked the story. Both of them were surprised when there were a couple of deep sighs from the water. They looked over and saw three mermaids were head and shoulders out of the water. The only way to tell them apart was their hair colour as their eyes all appeared the same. One was brunette, one was greenish-blond, and the third one was dark red.

"Love is sooo sweet," the greenish-blond one said. Her voice was high-pitched with a bubbling quality.

"It is," the red haired one said with a sigh.

"You were the ones who saved us," Prince Yester said.

"We usually are," the greenish-blond one said with a giggle, "So many people fall off those ships and we do not want so many to go see Jones."

"Who is Jones?" Valda asked.

"He collects the souls of those who die at sea," Prince Yester answered.

"Pretty much," the red one said, "But he likes the bodies as well as he uses them as well."

"You look familiar," the brunette one said tilting her

head to look at Prince Yester.

"I have never met a mermaid before," Prince Yester said, "I know more about them from stories my mother would tell me."

"That would be why you look familiar," the brunette said as she brightened, but then she did not explain further.

"What do you mean?" Prince Yester asked.

"Your mother," the brunette answered.

Prince Yester still looked confused. Valda did not understand the mermaid either. The mermaids all seemed to understand.

"What do you mean?" Prince Yester asked again.

"Your mother used to be a mermaid," the red one said, "She decided to become mostly human after she met your father."

"Mostly human?" Valda asked.

"Mermaids may change form and take on human characteristics, but we cannot be changed completely human," the red one answered, "For one thing, we live much longer than humans and no one can magic that part away."

"When would my father meet a mermaid?" Prince Yester asked.

"We do not know," the red one answered, "She had been disappearing a lot for several weeks and then when she came back she requested a chance at love, which meant becoming humanish."

"Do you know more stories?" the greenish-blond one asked, "We like stories but mermaids are not storytellers."

"I do know more stories," Prince Yester said, "But we need help getting to Yester. Maybe you can help us in exchange for stories."

The mermaids looked at each other. It was almost like they were talking without moving their mouths or making any noise. Finally, they nodded to each other.

"We can see what we can do to help you," the red one said, "But we are not supposed to go anywhere civilized by humans and the ship that was carrying you was pushed too far away to reach the islands."

"Is there another way to get back?" Prince Yester asked.

"Can you swim?" the brunette asked.

Prince Yester looked at Valda and she nodded.

"Yes," Prince Yester answered.

"Maybe we can help you swim between islands until you get to the island closest to Yester," the brunette said, "Because once you are there, it is easier to flag down a ship."

"That should work," Prince Yester said.

THE MERMAID PLAN AND WHAT COULD GO WRONG

"Since we heard a story, we will help you get to the next island," the red one said, "Are you ready?"

"I need a minute," Valda said, "I cannot swim in a long dress."

Valda got up and pulled off her gown. Prince Yester looked away. With her petticoats, Valda ripped them off at her knees.

"Now I am ready," Valda said.

"This way," the red one said as she waved for Prince Yester and Valda to enter the water. They waded into the water. The mermaids swam and they followed. Valda was not quite as fast as Prince Yester, but she kept him in sight.

It was a long way between islands and there was a short period where Prince Yester and Valda stayed in one place. Then they went back to following the mermaids again. The mermaids had waited for them.

By the time the next island was visible, Valda could feel exhaustion creeping up on her. When she managed to get her legs underneath her, Valda had trouble getting up off her knees to get the rest of the way on to the island. Prince Yester had noticed and he came to help her. Together they stumbled on to the sand.

"We will see you tomorrow," the red haired mermaid called.

Prince Yester and Valda waved. The mermaids swam away. Valda sat under one of the six trees on the island. Prince Yester gathered some of the fruit from the trees before joining her. They did not say anything as they ate the fruit. Only when they were finished and sitting there did Valda ask her question.

"How are you on finding out your mother is humanish and used to be a mermaid?" Valda asked.

"At first surprised," Prince Yester answered, "But now that I have thought about it, it makes sense with who she is. She did tell stories, but she was never as good at it as my father. She liked swimming, but did not stay long in sea water. She seemed sad when she had to get out of the water, however, she would not stay longer no matter how much I begged."

"I wonder if that means you are part mermaid," Valda said.

"Somehow I do not think so," Prince Yester said, "As much as I liked swimming and sailing, I do not feel much connection to the water. I think if I were part mermaid I would feel more connected to the water."

"My father said we had dwarf blood in our line," Valda said, "But it is pretty far back in the line that it hardly seems to matter."

"Dwarves are story characters in Yester," Prince

Yester said.

"Mermaids are similar in Proster," Valda said, "Makes sense as it seems if people did not see certain creatures regularly they start to think them to be myths."

"True," Prince Yester said, "I suppose we tell stories to remind us they are not myths."

"I was wondering if the stories about the islands were written down somewhere," Valda said, "Because I would love to know the rest of them."

"I do not believe they are," Prince Yester said, "But occasionally, I have thought of writing them down."

"Maybe when we get to Yester, you could try," Valda said.

"Sounds like a good idea," Prince Yester said. He smiled at her and she smiled back. They were quiet for several minutes. Valda looked out over the water for several minutes.

"Are you okay?" Prince Yester asked. She looked at him and saw his concern.

"I am," Valda answered, "I do not mind adventures."

"Adventures are not the most comfortable of things," Prince Yester said.

"That is true," Valda said, "And almost drowning is not what I call fun, but we spent the day swimming with mermaids and that part was okay."

Prince Yester nodded.

"And we are not without hope of getting out of our situation," Valda said.

"I might have to ask the mermaids what type of story they want to hear," Prince Yester said, "Because they may not want to hear just the stories about the islands."

"They may already know them," Valda said.

"Growing up I always thought the stories were like the myths," Prince Yester said, "But I am beginning to think they may not be. I had never connected the fact that in the story the nobleman's daughter gave the king the dragon's tear and the crown had a dragon's tear in it. I think I might even know which noble family they were part of."

"Do you think they tell the story about how their parents met?" Valda asked.

"Based on what I know of the current generation, no, they do not," Prince Yester answered, "I think their children might have gotten too much from her father and not enough from them. They prefer business matters over less so-called practical matters."

"They are missing so much by focusing on those matters," Valda said, "Not that they should ignore those, but stories are important too."

"I agree," Prince Yester said, "But there are some people who do not understand."

Valda nodded. She found herself yawning, even though she had not thought herself to be tired.

"Sleep," Prince Yester said, "We can talk again tomorrow and we also have to be up to more swimming."

"Okay," Valda said as she did not feel like arguing. She curled up in the sand and closed her eyes. Valda was sure she would take a few minutes to fall asleep, but she did not remember lying there awake.

The sun woke Valda up. It was rising. Prince Yester was not awake yet and there were no mermaids in sight. Valda did find herself pressed against Prince Yester, but she did not mind much as he was warm and it helped her stay warm. She did not move as she did not want to lose that. Instead, her mind started.

Valda wondered about her decision to travel to see where Prince Yester lived to see whether he was the same man as when he was travelling. She now believed he was the same no matter where he was. Now she was not sure she would have been able to get home, even if he did not turn out to the man she had hoped he would be. She was not sure she would be able to send a message home to say she had arrived, though they must have successful journeys across the ocean based on stories and things Prince Yester had said about trade.

There was some movement from Prince Yester, but then he was still. Valda glanced at him and found he had woken up. But he did not seem to want to move any more than she did. She did not move and left him alone.

"The majority of trips between Yester and the main land do not end up in losing people off the ships," Prince Yester said, "If you decide you want to go home, it is safe to do so."

"Do you want me to go?" Valda asked.

"No, I would like it if you stayed," Prince Yester answered, "But I do not want to keep you here if you would rather go."

"As much as I love my family and I will miss them," Valda said, "I think I want to stay."

"Good," Prince Yester said.

Before they could say anything else, they heard splashing from nearby. Valda looked over and saw the mermaids were coming towards them. She and Prince Yester finally sat up.

The three mermaids stopped before the water got too

shallow for them.

"We really want to hear the story," the red one said, "But it might be best to hear it when we reach the next island as it will take longer to get there."

"Then we should get going," Prince Yester said. He and Valda got up and waded into the water. They followed the mermaids. Once again Valda found herself falling behind, however, she could see Prince Yester ahead of her in the water and could continue to follow them.

About noonish, the mermaids found a sandbar for Prince Yester and Valda to rest on. The mermaids also offered them some kelp to eat. Prince Yester and Valda tried it, but found they were unable to eat more than one piece. It was enough to keep their stomachs from complaining too much. When they were rested, they got back into the water to follow the mermaids to the island.

Valda quickly found herself falling behind, but she could still see Prince Yester so she was not worried. Her concentration was on swimming and keeping him in sight. Because of that she did not notice when she swam over something dark in the water. Valda let out a squeak of surprise when the dark thing rose and she was wrapped in something. It pulled her right out of the water.

As Valda was hanging there, she realized she had been caught in a fishing net and was being taken on board a ship. Several members of the crew of the ship were at the railing reaching out with eager hands to guide the net. They did not look like any of the sailors from the ship she and Prince Yester had been sailing on. Instead, these men appeared more rough and ragged. A chill ran through Valda as she realized these were pirates.

Valda had read enough about pirates to know how dangerous they were and it was never a good thing to be captured by them, especially if one was a woman. Some of Prince Yester's stories involved pirates and the pirates were always the villains. But it was best if she did not panic and instead figured out a way to get away from them. It would be better if she could get away from them because Valda was unsure when Prince Yester and the mermaids would notice when she was missing and try to figure out what happened to her. They might never find her because once on board, the ship could disappear and they would never realize there had been a ship around.

The hands grasped the net and guided it to the deck of the ship. Suddenly something was released and Valda felt herself falling. The wooden boards of the ship deck were a hard landing and caused her to lose her breath. There was laughter coming from the men nearby. Valda looked around and saw so many men crowding around. One on the higher deck must have been the captain because his clothing seemed to be of better quality than the rest.

"That is not a mermaid," the captain's voice was loud enough to be heard over everything else, "You were supposed to catch a mermaid."

"Who else would be swimming out this far out?" one of the men closer to Valda asked. He had a pole in his hands and looked at Valda as if he was expecting a response. Valda could feel that she was able to breathe again but she did not answer him. He used to end of the pole to poke her in the side.

"Answer," he said.

"I was swimming to the next island in hopes of finding a ship to take me to Yester," Valda answered.

"She swims," the man with the pole called up to the captain.

"Maybe we can use her," the captain said.

The crowd of pirates started to disperse, except two who came over and wrapped her wrists and ankles in ropes. They attached the ends of the ropes to the main mast so she could not get away. Valda wiggled until she was in the shade of the mast rather than directly in the sunlight.

At first Valda was not as scared because they obviously had a use for her and that in her mind meant they would not hurt her, but the looks from those pirates who went by her caused the fear to come back. She leaned against the mast and tried to ignore it. As tired as Valda was, she was unable to sleep. She wondered how long it would take before Prince Yester and the mermaids would miss her. She hoped it would not take until they reached the next island as it would make it harder to figure out where she went and the come to rescue her.

Valda was not one to wait for someone else to rescue her, but she was not sure how to get out of the situation. She could not move her legs as they were tied too tight. Valda could move her wrists slightly, but it was not enough for her to loosen them. Even if she could get free, Valda was not sure how to get off the ship. It was a long drop to just jump off the ship and she might not survive it. None of the pirates looked friendly enough to ask for help and she was not sure any of them would be willing to go against the crew. Since she did not know what they needed her for, aside from something involving swimming, it was hard to figure out if she could get any of them to help her.

Based on the stories, Valda knew they were motivated by greed and lust. Since they had not touched her, she figured what they wanted involved greed. She had nothing to offer in exchange and especially since she did not know what they were searching for. Telling them that she was a princess and going to Yester with the prince would not help her in the situation. She was sure of that.

Prince Yester stopped and treated water for several minutes. He looked around as he had not been able to hear Princess Vada for several minutes. Her head was not visible as it usually was when he checked.

"Valda?" Prince Yester shouted. There was no response, nor did she pop up in the water. But the mermaids stopped and came back towards him. He stayed in one place. When the mermaids reached him, they went passed him to look for Valda. But they back soon.

"She is gone," the red one said.

"We need to find her," Prince Yester said. He started swimming back the way they had come. The mermaids swam with him. There was no sign of what happened to her. The brunette mermaid went ahead.

Several minutes later the brunette mermaid came back. Prince Yester stopped his forward movement so he could hear what she had to say.

"There is a ship moving away," the brunette said, "She may have been taken on board that."

"It is likely a pirate ship," the red mermaid said.

"We will not be able to catch up to the ship," Prince Yester said.

"The ship is headed away from the islands," the brunette mermaid said.

"What is out there?" Prince Yester asked.

"There are a few larger islands," the brunette answered, "But we did not go out there as creatures that live out there eat mermaids."

"Is there a faster way to follow the ship?" Prince Yester asked.

"Unless you can request a ride from a whale or dolphin, not really," the red mermaid answered, "They did not like to do such."

"Is it far?" Prince Yester asked, "Because I cannot swim as far or as fast as you three."

"We can ask," the greenish-blond mermaid said before she disappeared under the water.

"Thank you," Prince Yester said. He started moving forward again. The other two mermaids continued along with him.

The sun was sinking below the horizon. Valda wondered if Prince Yester and the mermaids had noticed she was missing yet. She was tired as the sun had been beating down on her for the last few hours and she could not move around the mast to get out of it. The pirates going by still leered at her, which still scared her. It had been a very long day.

Valda wanted to go home at this moment. As much as she had enjoyed swimming with mermaids and spending time with Prince Yester, being captured by pirates had been very uncomfortable. She was missing her own bed, her family, and not being on a pirate ship surrounded by pirates; though Aldous would probably love to hear the story of this adventure. She might have to write it down and send it to him if she survived and was rescued.

The sun was gone and she was trapped in the darkness of the night. There were a couple lanterns lit and hung on each end of the ship. Most of the crew went below for the night leaving a limited amount of deck. None of them bothered with Valda. It was like she was part of the mast and not a captive of them. Some ways she appreciated it and other ways she would have liked a drink or some food.

Valda's feet had gone numb, but her hands still had feeling in them. Unfortunately, she could not move her legs and feet enough. Her back against the wooden deck was not comfortable either. She really would have rather been anywhere else than the position she was currently in. At home in her own bed being the best option. But it was not happening as she was not likely to see her own home again, even if she was rescued from the pirates.

She blinked a few times as she was starting to be tired enough to sleep. No one had walked by her since most of them went below. Valda did not think she was currently in danger as the captain seemed to have told all of the crew not to touch her, however, she was unsure how well pirates paid attention to orders from their captain. Those thoughts caused Valda to feel panicky and desperate to get out of there.

Valda brought her wrists to her mouth and tried to pull the knots apart with her teeth. They were very tight and it was difficult to get any movement out of the rope. She tried pulling her wrists apart, but it did not help. No matter how she struggled and bit the rope, the knot did not budge. Her muscles complained and she had to stop. With a sigh, Valda felt like she had to give up. She might as well sleep. Valda let her eyes close.

Prince Yester was tired but he knew that he could not stop and rest. The greenish-blond mermaid had come back with a dolphin, who was willing to give him a ride. He was glad for that but they had not managed to catch up with the ship. When night had fallen, the dolphin had to go and Prince Yester had to go back to swimming himself. The mermaids were still swimming with him and trying to keep him going and in the right direction.

But when they came upon a sandbar, Prince Yester had to stop to rest because his muscles wanted to give up on him. The mermaids gave him another piece of kelp to eat and he had but there was nothing else to eat. He wanted to sleep because he was thirsty, hungry, and tired. As much as he wanted to finish the voyage home and then come back with re-enforcements, he knew it would be difficult to find the ship and thus harder to rescue Princess Valda. He really wanted to rescue Princess Valda. Prince Yester could not see the rest of his life without her, especially after she told him she was willing to stay with him after ending up lost on an island.

Those thoughts made him get up and go back into the water. The mermaids had been waiting and they swam with him. He appreciated their presence as it kept him on the right course. Prince Yester was pretty sure they would not be as helpful about rescuing Princess Valda as they did not have any reason to help him do that as they likely already felt owed for what they had done. Since they wanted stories, Prince Yester was not as worried about the payments. But he wanted Princess Valda by his side before he provided the stories.

Valda woke when the sun touched the deck. The crew were coming up from below and taking up their positions again. She remembered exactly where she was and there was no transition as she became aware of the world. There was just the fear going through her at the sight of the pirates. The difference of this day from the previous day was that the captain came out and stood on the higher deck near the wheel where he could supervise what was happening. Valda assumed that meant the ship was getting close to their destination.

She pushed the panic down as she knew they wanted her to swim somewhere and it was unlikely to hurt her before then. But with limited sleep, no food, and nothing to drink it was hard not to go straight to the instinct of fear and panic. The crew ignored her as they focused on their jobs. Valda wished Prince Yester was there because then even though they were in danger they would be in it together.

Suddenly the captain started shouting orders. The man, who had been using the pole when Valda was first brought on board, came over with another man and they untied her from the mast but did not untie her. They carried her to the long boat and put her inside. The long boat was lowered over the side and into the water. The two men got into the long boat along with a couple of others. They pushed off from the ship. There were a couple other long boats with them.

Valda could not see over the side of the boat and

thus could not see where they were headed. She hoped they were not just going to throw her over the side and expect her to swim. If they did, she would likely sink rather than swim as her legs were not likely to work. Not only that but her arm muscles had been cramping up.

The long boat hit land and the pirates climbed out to pull the boat the rest of the way. Then the man took the rope off her ankles before pulling her out of the boat. Valda felt the sand as it rushed up to meet her as her legs were not going to hold her. The man stood over her, but did not try to get her up again. The other long boats were still on the way. Valda used the time to stretch her legs and get the circulation back. She still did not have much movement in her hands as the man had not removed the rope from her wrists.

The next few long boats reached the land and the pirates got out. The captain was in the last long boat. Once he was standing in the sand, the pirates got organized and ready to move forward. The man grabbed Valda under the arm and pulled her to her feet. This time she was able to stand and walk. For the first time, Valda noticed where they were. There was sand to a tree line and then there were rock walls preventing her from seeing anything else. They headed into the rock walls with the captain leading the party. The man kept his hand on Valda and pushed her forward.

They walked through the rock walls for a long time before it opened up into a larger area with a pool of water in the centre. The pirates all stopped far enough from the edge that they would not fall in. When she was close enough, Valda could see it was a deep pool. The man took the rope off Valda's wrists and let her massage the circulation back.

"There are two keys in the bottom of this pool," the captain said, "You will retrieve both of them for us."

Valda nodded but she was not sure how she was going get the keys. The water was clear, so she should be able to see. It was the diving and staying down long enough to find them. But they were not giving her a chance to back down or say no. When Valda thought she could actually swim, she stepped into the water. The first couple of steps were okay, but then the next one was over her head. She kept her head above water for a moment. It was fresh water. She took a deep breath and then went down.

It was not as clear as it has looked from above but she could see things fairly well. Once at the bottom, Valda only had a short time to look around before she had to head back to the surface for air. The bottom was sand and that made it more difficult to find the keys. However, Valda thought she saw something to one side of the pool. After she had exchanged the air, she swam over to it. She grasped whatever the object was and then had to get to the surface for more air.

The item was indeed a key. It was not a regular key as it was heavy and it gleamed as if from within rather than the sunlight hitting it.

"Give it here," the captain said.

Valda was unsure what else to do as she could not hide them and did not know what the keys were for. So, she swam over to where the captain was leaning over the water. She held the key out of the water towards him. He snatched the key. The pirates around him sat up and were now paying more attention to what was going on. Whatever these keys were they were important and valuable.

In an attempt to see the other key, Valda looked down at the bottom of the pool. She could not see any other objects from that view point. So, she took a deep breath and went down. She looked around at the sand, but she did not see anything before she had to get air again.

"Keep looking," the captain said.

Valda did not stop to listen to the captain as she took another deep breath and went back down again. She touched the sand but did not get far before needing more air. Since she seemed to be following orders, the captain did not give her any more. Valda went back down and tried to work from where she had been before.

She went back down again and again. Valda sifted through the sand with her hands, but she could not feel the key. She looked around and could not see it either. It was frustrating as she felt it should not be so hard to find this second key. The captain and other pirates were also feeling the same as they would yell at her when she would come up for air.

Valda went under the surface so it was harder to hear the pirates. She looked down at the bottom. Nothing was visible in the sand at the bottom. It had been stirred up but had already settled. If there was something down there, Valda would have found it. So, where could this key be? She looked around, not only at the bottom but also at the rock walls around it.

Half-way up the rock wall was something. Valda surfaced long enough to get another breath of air. She went down towards where the object was and felt around on the rock. There was a little bit of an alcove in the rock and the key was mostly inside. She was able to grab the key and then headed for the surface.

"Bring it here," the captain said.

Valda did not have any other choice than to swim over and hold the key up for the captain. He snatched the key and then grabbed her arm. She was pulled out of the water and then the man re-tied the rope around her wrists. Then he gripped her upper arm and they followed the captain back towards the beach with the rest of the crewmembers following.

When they arrived at the beach, she was put into the long boat. The long boat was pushed into the water and the men got into the boat. Once again, Valda could not see over the side of the boat but she was sure they were heading back to the ship. It was not long before the boat hit something gently. The men moved and got out, but they left her inside the boat for now. The long boat was hauled up on the ship, at which point the man pulled her out.

Valda was now was scared about what they were going to do with her. That they needed her for something had been what protected her. Now they did not. Nothing would stop them from doing whatever they wanted, not unless she could think up some way to convince them not to. Unfortunately, she could not think of anything.

The man pulled Valda out of the long boat. Everyone was hurrying off to their jobs on the ship as all the boats appeared to be on board and getting ready to sail. The man dragged Valda down the stairs below the deck. She did not try to fight him as she did not know what he was going to do. He took her over to where the cargo was stored. One of the crates was opened. The man forced Valda into the crate and he closed the lid on her. She could hear him hammering the lid on.

Valda could not see out but a small amount of light came through the cracks in the crate. There was enough room for her to shift positions, but it was not comfortable to rest against the sides or the bottom. She could hear the man walking away. Valda could also hear the crew on deck and the water against the side. But she really did not know what was happening outside the crate. With a sigh, she settled in as she was not sure how long she was going to be stuck in there.

Prince Yester was trying to catch his breath. The mermaids were still swimming with him, but they were used to swimming while this was most swimming he had done in years. He had taken a short nap on the last sandbar because he had thought he might collapse from exhaustion if he did not. As much as he really wanted to save Valda, there was only so much he could do physically.

Now the ship was in sight and he did not want to try to get on board while he was too tired to fight. Since the ship was anchored near an island, Prince Yester thought he had time. The mermaid could not answer anything about the island as it would outside their usual travel area. Since they could not tell him anything, he did not want to try to go into an unknown situation tired.

Prince Yester was trying to get his muscles to work for him when he saw the long boat coming back to the ship. He searched but could not see Princess Valda in the boats. He wanted to ask the mermaids whether they were sure about Princess Valda being on board this ship, however, there was a bigger problem he had to face. If the ship sailed away without him, Prince Yester was sure he would never succeed at rescuing Princess Valda as swimming after a ship is foolishness even if one could swim like a mermaid.

He moved forward while staying low in the water to not be noticeable to anyone who might be watching on the ship. The mermaids did not follow him, but watched him go. Prince Yester moved around to the opposite side than where the long boats were headed. It meant he could not see the activity, but if he stopped and listened he could hear some of it. However, he did not want to stop often or long as he did not know when they would start moving.

This worry became much more real when Prince Yester was almost to the ship when it started to move. He sped up while still trying to not attract attention from those on board. Reaching out, Prince Yester tattempted to grab onto the ship. He almost got a grip on it when it moved away. The ship must have caught the wind as Prince Yester struggled to get close enough to grab on. He needed to get on that ship.

Suddenly two of the mermaids were on either side of him. They each took a side and pushed him the distance to the ship. He was able to grab on and hold. Prince Yester got his footing on the side and pulled himself up into a squat. He waved a thank you to the mermaids and they waved back. They would go back to their usual area and then find him for their payment if he survived.

The wood of the ship was slippery and the ship was picking up speed. Prince Yester tried to move up enough for him to be sure of not falling off. It was a struggle to keep himself up, let alone climb, as his muscles did not want to cooperate. They were shaking and trying to give out. Prince Yester took a deep breath to steady himself and then hauled himself to a place where he could sit without being seen. His muscles still complained and were going limp, but he was not in danger of falling off the ship which was the important part.

Prince Yester did want to get himself the rest of the way on the ship, so he could search for Princess Valda. However, physically he was not able to move. He might have thought about sleeping until he had the energy, but he would have to settle for resting in place as sleeping might cause him to fall off. The sun beat down drying his clothing and making them stiff. Prince Yester wondered if this situation made Princess Valda not appreciate being on an adventure as much as she had been before.

The slowing down of the ship caused Prince Yester to come back to his current situation. He looked around and saw the sun was now half-way to the horizon. Ahead of the ship was an island with a large tower made of stones surrounded by trees and smaller buildings. There was a sandy beach between the water and trees. It looked like a good place for a hideout.

The ship stopped and the anchor was lowered. The water around the island appeared to be shallow, so the ship really could not have gotten any closer. Prince Yester would hear the long boat being put into the water. He was not sure what to do next as he could not see the long boats. Whether he should wait and search the ship or drop into the water and follow the sailors were thoughts tumbling through Prince Yester's mind.

To figure out what was going on, Prince Yester climbed the side of the ship so he could peer onto the deck. The sailors were much rougher looking than most he knew and he realized they were pirates. They were busy bringing crates up from below to transport them to the island. There did not seem to be any area where anyone was being held captive as no sailors were standing around on watch. Prince Yester wondered if Princess Valda was already in one of the long boats. It would make sense to take any prisoner to the island before worrying about cargo.

Prince Yester could not get around to see the long boats from his position. He ducked down to avoid being seen. The first long boat launched from the ship was visible at the front of the ship. There were several pirates inside but no one else. Prince Yester was not sure if he should have been worried about not seeing Princess Valda. If she was a prisoner, why was she not being transported to the island?

He could hear the movement of the cargo on the ship by the crew. Prince Yester peered over the edge of the ship again because he decided it was best to see what was going on. They were moving crates to the side so they could put them on the boats. The captain stood there over seeing it all, but did not give any orders. The crew seemed to already know what they were supposed to be doing and did it without prompting.

It was almost dark by the time the crew had moved the cargo into the long boats and sent it to the island. The last long boat took the captain to the island. No one was left on the ship, even as watch. Prince Yester waited until the long boat was half-way to the island before he climbed on deck. He could not see anyone on deck, but Prince Yester wandered it just to be sure no one was there. No one was there.

Prince Yester went below deck and searched for any sign of Princess Valda. Or even any sign of captives. There was none, as there was no cargo. There was nothing, except some basic supplies the pirates would need the next time they went off. Prince Yester reached the captain's cabin and looked inside. Everything left there were things found in every captain's cabin. Nothing to tell him where Princess Valda was.

Getting back on deck, Prince Yester looked around again but he did not see anything he had not seen before. He climbed down the side of the ship and slipped into the water. He followed the long boats across the water to the island. The long boats were lined up on the sand ready to be filled and pushed back into the water, however, none of the pirates were left on the beach.

Prince Yester followed the footprints in the sand into a path between the trees. He was careful of anyone else moving along the path. It led him through the trees to what appeared to be a small village of wooden huts. This is where Prince Yester found most of the pirates. He kept hidden from view while studying things. The pirates were reacting like most people do when they arrived home. Prince Yester did not see any people aside from the pirates. If there were anyone else on this island, they were not visible. The path forked with one branch heading into the village and the other going off towards the stone tower. One side of the path were trees, so Prince Yester could go along it in the trees without being seen.

No one else was travelling along this path making it

easier for Prince Yester to move without being seen. It was not long before he reached the end of the trees and was just a short reach to the tower. Two pirates were standing in the doorway, while the another was going going through one of the crates sitting near the doorway. They were mumbling to each other, but it was not loud enough for Prince Yester to hear what they were saying.

Rather than try to get in this guarded entrance, Prince Yester stayed in the trees and moved around the tower. It was large enough to house a banquet hall and there was a window mid-way up with several more at equal intervals up from there. Prince Yester could not see anything in the windows. He also could not hear any noise from them. He reached the other side of the tower, but there was no door on this side. Rather than go back, he continued around.

Prince Yester reached the end of the trees. He would have to cross the path to make it the rest of the way and he did not bother as he could see the doorway and the pirates from where he was. They did not seem to be in any hurry to do anything more than stand around and they were between him and being able to search the tower. Prince Yester sat down and leaned against a tree while he tried to figure out what to do next.

The box was not comfortable to start with and while it was being moved, Valda found it worse. She tried not to move, but it was hard when the crate was tipped either direction. The pirates hauled the crate around as if they did not know she was inside. But then she was not sure if they did or not. The crate might as well have held bolts of cloth with the way they were moving it and she was trying not to end up with too many bruises at the treatment.

The crate was set down. Valda was not sure what to expect now. She wondered if they were going to open the crate or leave it alone. She could hear the conversation, but, aside from some orders being shouted at them the, pirates were not speaking any language Valda knew. They laughed with each other and talked, however, she could not understand what was happening. The crate was not opened by the pirates and Valda could even feel another crate being placed on top. There were three placed on each side, but the fourth side was left without one. Light came through that side.

There were some more noises and then she could hear all the pirates leave the area. She listened, but wherever they went she could no longer hear them. Valda tried to push against the sides of the crate, however, the crate was well made and nothing was going to move. She did not want to knock against the sides as she did not want to draw attention to herself as who knew what they would do to her. Realizing she could not do anything for herself at the moment, Valda tried to get comfortable while she waited until she might be able to escape.

Prince Yester blinked. Slowly he realized he was sitting under a tree and it was night. The light he saw by was a lantern hanging by the doorway to the tower. Worry for Princess Valda went through his mind, but he was still unsure how to find her and rescue her at this point. However, he did see that the tower's entrance was no longer guarded by any of the pirates.

He got to his feet and moved forward carefully. No one appeared to be around. Prince Yester reached the entrance without being accosted by any of the pirates. The door was not locked and opened easily for him. Inside was a large room and it was filled with a huge table. To one side was a large, unlit hearth. Near the door was a staircase heading up. That was everything in the room and there were no pirates in sight.

There was little other choice for Prince Yester, he headed up the stairs. He moved much more slowly than he really wanted because he listened for anyone else along the stairs. The stairs went around the outside of the tower as they went up. When Prince Yester reached the first window, it was at a landing with a closed door and the stairs continuing up. He stopped and went to the door. It was not locked and opened when he tried. There was a lantern lit and sitting on a desk on one side of the room. The rest of the room was filled with furniture as if it was someone's living quarters. Whoever it was, they were not here.

Prince Yester stepped into the room and looked around. There was no place to hide a person and no signs of a captive. Based on the clothing in the room, this was the captain's residence. Prince Yester was just about to leave the room when his eyes fell on the book sitting on the desk. He went over and looked closer at it. The title across the cover in gold was Fabled Gardens. Prince Yester turned to the page marked with the ribbon. The type at the top of the page announced the Tree of Immortality and then below was a drawing of a tree. It appeared to be an apple tree. There was a description of the tree, which guarded by great monsters and almost impossible to reach if a person had not already eaten an apple from the tree. Apples from the tree do not rot, so those who did get through would take multiple to sell or give to others.

Prince Yester closed the book. He moved away from the desk. A sound from the doorway caused him to turn and look. The captain was standing there with several pirates behind him and all with their weapons out.

"And what do we have here?" the captain asked.

"Looks like someone in need of punishment for trespassing," the one pirate answered.

"I am looking for the woman I was courting," Prince Yester said, "Otherwise, I would not be here."

"And why should we give her back?" the captain asked, "She was captured by us and thus rightfully ours."

"She was travelling with me," Prince Yester answered, "Capture does not mean right of ownership."

"What stops us from killing you?" the captain asked.

"Because if I do not return home, people will come searching for me and will destroy anyone who has harmed me," Prince Yester answered.

"I suppose we should listen to such threats," the captain said. The pirates behind him looked slightly surprised, but Prince Yester could hear the lack of seriousness in the captain's voice.

"But we cannot just hand over the woman," the captain said, "We will escort you down while I decide what it will take for such a thing to happen."

Prince Yester did not say anything. Two pirates entered the room and each took one of Prince Yester's arms. They took him out and down the stairs. He did not fight them as he hoped whatever the captain thought up would be something he could win and then they would just hand over Princess Valda. It would mean he did not have to keep searching for her. The captain and the pirates followed them down the stairs.

When they reached the bottom, the pirates sat Prince Yester down at the table. The captain sat down across the table from him.

"I be Captain Lang," the captain said, "Who be you?"

"Ernest," Prince Yester answered.

"Noble blood?" the captain asked.

"From Yester," Prince Yester answered with a nod.

"Better at finding things at sea," the captain said, "You threat might have weight. What be fair?"

Prince Yester did not say anything. The pirates around them did not hold back on their suggestions. The captain listened to the overlapping voices for several minutes before holding up his hand. The pirates fell silent immediately.

"How about dice?" the captain asked with a smile. Several dark teeth were visible.

"If you must," Prince Yester answered. He knew that games of dice were disapproved of by the nobility and the captain expected the same of him. Prince Yester did his best not to give anything away. The pirates laughed as they expected Prince Yester to lose. The captain took out a handful of dice and set them on the table. As much as he knew it best to play with his own dice, Prince Yester did not have any to offer and thus he would have to play with the captain's dice. Someone set a mug on the table.

The captain loaded his dice into the mug and shook it. When he was ready, the captain poured the dice out on the table. It was a good roll. Prince Yester waited until the captain nodded to him before putting the dice back into the mug and shook it. He poured the dice onto the table. The dice were not as nice to him as they have been for the captain, however, it was not enough to lose.

The captain frowned at them because he had hoped Prince Yester would lose so quickly. He gathered the dice into the mug for his turn. When the dice landed on the table, they gave another good roll. The pirates around them cheered. Prince Yester gathered the dice and put them into the mug. He shook it and then poured the dice onto the table. It was not a good roll, but once again it was not a complete loss.

There was a humph from the captain before he took his turn. Prince Yester watched the result of the roll. The pirates were pleased enough to shout. The captain was not happy with Prince Yester's roll, but nothing he could do except take his own turn. It was a good roll and would be close to a winning one. Prince Yester took his turn and did not lose the game again.

There was a feeling of frustration starting to come off the captain. Prince Yester knew he needed to win this game, or the punishment might be far greater than he wanted. If he angered the captain too much the threat of future pain would not mean anything. But the dice did not seem to be willing to let either of them win.

Prince Yester was used to his luck being enough to have things go in his favour, but these were the captain's dice and the captain had enough luck of his own. It made for a stale mate. Prince Yester tried to think of some way to tip luck to his side. If he had his own dice it would have helped a lot, but he did not. He tried to think of something else. The only thing that came to mind was if Princess Valda had any luck connected to her. He was not sure whether he could borrow any of it, but he was sure her family must have plenty otherwise, the kingdom of Proster would not have been so prosperous.

The captain was getting cheers from the pirates around them, despite him not winning and the game dragging on. Someone on his crew must be trying to get more luck in the captain's direction. Prince Yester tried to concentrate without bringing any attention to what he was doing. The captain took his turn and received similar rolls to what he had been getting so far. Prince Yester let everyone see the dice before he touched them. He put them in the mug and tried to get luck to be on his side. Then he shook the mug and then tipped it so the dice rolled out. It was the same situation as the last roll.

Prince Yester worked very hard not to sigh as he was also getting tired of how long this game was going on. The captain barely allowed people to see what Prince Yester rolled before gathering the dice up for his turn. He shook the mug with vigour and then poured the dice out. It did not change the type of roll he got. Prince Yester left the dice alone for a moment before putting them back into the mug. He did not try to gather the luck to him this time, instead, he breathed as much tension out as possible. Shaking the mug, Prince Yester then rolled the dice onto the table.

The dice gave him a winning hand. It was higher than the one the captain had rolled. Prince Yester let himself smile a little bit. The captain tightened his fist in anger; he was not happy with the result.

"I won," Prince Yester said, "You will give her back

now."

"I did agree to that, did I not?" the captain asked.

"You did," Prince Yester answered. "Are you going back on your word? I would have thought you were a more honourable man than that."

"I did agree," the captain said, "Let us go get her."

The captain got to his feet and Prince Yester did the same. They went back up the stairs with the rest of the pirates following them. They went passed the door to the captain's residence. When they came upon the next window, it was another landing with another door. The captain stopped on this landing and he opened the door. Inside were stacks of crates. This must have been where they were keeping the cargo from the ship. The pirates entered the room and then they started taking the crates down from the nearest pile.

When they reached the bottom crate, the captain pulled the top off. Princess Valda sat up and looked around. She was bruised and confused as to what was happening. The captain offered her a hand out of the crate, which she accepted with further confusion. She climbed out. Then she ran over to Prince Yester and hugged him. He wrapped his arms around her and was relieved that she did not seem to be injured. Prince Yester did not want to let go, ever, but he knew that they needed to get away from the pirates.

"As I agreed, you won her," the captain said.

"I did," Prince Yester said. He could feel Princess Valda's confusion but he would explain later.

"But I did not agree to let you both go," the captain said, "Take them below."

Prince Yester and Princess Valda had their hands tied behind their backs and then they were taken down the stairs. But the pirates did not stop at the large room at the bottom, instead, a trap door was opened and they were forced through it. None of the pirates went with them and instead, once they were inside the trap door was closed. It cut off all the light from the large room.

Valda was not sure what to do as she could not see anything and the only thing she could feel was the stone of the stairs beneath her feet. She could hear Prince Yester moving beside her. He seemed to be going down the stairs. Above they could hear the pirates leaving.

"What is happening?" Valda asked. She found her voice hoarse as she had not had anything to drink since she retrieved the keys.

"The mermaids helped me follow the ship once we realized you had been captured," Prince Yester answered, "And I then caught a ride the rest of the way to this island where the pirates have a hideout. I was searching for you when I was caught by the pirates and the captain agreed to let me have you if I could win against him with dice, which I did. Now we need to figure out how to get out of here. Why did they capture you?"

"They were hoping to get a mermaid," Valda answered, "They got me to retrieve some keys from the bottom of a pool on a different island. I do not know what the keys are for, or anything else because they were speaking another language."

"I have heard the language, but I do not know it," Prince Yester said, "But I may know what is locked up that they want. There was a book in the captain's room about a tree with apples that can make a person immortal."

"How are keys going to get them to a tree?" Valda asked.

"I think there is one apple locked up somewhere," Prince Yester answered.

"Would it not go bad?" Valda asked.

"Apparently not," Prince Yester answered.

"That cannot be good for anyone who would hunt the pirates," Valda said.

"No, it would not," Prince Yester said.

"How are we going to get out of here?" Valda asked, "I cannot see anything."

"I am trying to feel my way around and if there is anything else here," Prince Yester answered, "But I am not finding much."

Valda stepped back towards the trap door until she could feel it at her back and she pushed, but the trap door did not move. Not being sure what else to do, Valda sat down on the stairs. She tried to free her hands.

"We should probably stop them from getting the apple," Valda said.

"Probably," Prince Yester's voice came from farther away than before. It echoed against the stone walls.

"It would help if we knew where it was locked up," Valda said, "They brought the keys back to their hideout, so maybe it is somewhere on the island. What does the island look like?"

"We are in a tower," Prince Yester said, "There is a small village nearby where the rest of the pirates live and then it is all surrounded by trees. Then there is a sand beach."

"Not many places to put an item and lock it up," Valda said.

"Not really," Prince Yester said, "But I was not able to search to the top of the tower."

There was a splashing sound.

"What was that?" Valda asked.

"I stepped in water," Prince Yester answered, "It seems to be a puddle on the floor." There was the sound of movement through the water.

"The water must be coming from somewhere," Valda said.

"It is getting deeper as I go farther," Prince Yester said, "I am going to keep going and hopefully, I will find the source."

"Okay," Valda said. She felt useless and she hated the feeling, but she was not sure what she could do. Valda did not know what to do as Prince Yester was already trying to figure out what was in the space and she could not get her hands free. With nothing else, she twisted her wrists and pulled at the rope. She tried to get at the knots with her fingers, but she could not do so.

Valda was concentrating so much on the ropes that she lost track of Prince Yester and what he was doing. When she finally gave up trying to get free, she listened but could no longer hear him. She thought about calling out, however, something in her gut suggested she not do so. Then she heard movement in the water again. It sounded to be at a distance and coming closer. Because she could not see anything and was not sure whether it was Prince Yester or something else, Valda could feel the fear going through her.

"Are you all right?" Prince Yester's voice came from the darkness.

"I am fine," Valda answered. The fear lessened its

grip on her.

"There is a hole in the wall at the far end," Prince Yester said, "But it is all flooded."

"Could we still get out that way?" Valda asked.

"I could not tell how far it went," Prince Yester answered, "I thought it best to come back for you first."

"I cannot get the rope from my wrist," Valda said.

"Come here and I will see if I can help," Prince Yester said.

Valda stood up and carefully moved down the stairs. When she ran out of stairs, Valda found Prince Yester standing at the bottom. He had managed to get the rope from his own wrists as he had the use of his hands. He used his sense of touch to untie the rope. It was not long before Valda felt the rope fall away.

"Thank you," Valda said. She took his hand in hers.

"This way," Prince Yester said. He pulled her away from the stairs and farther into the tower cellar. It was not very far before Valda could feel herself step into the water. It was cold against her skin. The next step took her deeper into the water. She could hear Prince Yester walking in the water in front of her.

Valda found herself waist deep in the water before Prince Yester stopped. Though she could not see it, Valda could feel something solid in front of them. It must have been the wall of the other side of the cellar. Prince Yester took Valda's hand and she felt him put it to the wall. He showed her where the hole in the wall was. Not only that, the hole was big enough for them to fit through.

"The island is fairly large," Prince Yester said, "If we have to swim the whole way to the sea, we will not have enough breath to make it."

"We might as well go," Valda said, "No one knows where we are and the trap door is not going to move."

"All right," Prince Yester said, "Let us go."

Valda could feel Prince Yester let go and move forward into the hole. She heard him go under. After taking a deep breath, Valda went under and felt her way into the hole in the wall. She used her hands to push her way through the tunnel. The water might have been moving into the cellar but there was no current.

It seemed like a long time, but it must not have been because her lungs were just starting to burn when Valda felt the end of the tunnel. She moved upward and her head broke the surface of the water. There was enough room for her whole head could be out of the water. She let out her breath and took in some new air. The air was slightly stale, but breathable.

"Valda?" Prince Yester asked from somewhere nearby.

"I am here," Valda answered, "Where are we?"

"I am not sure," Prince Yester said.

Valda put her feet down and found she could stand up. The water only came up to her chest. It did not sound like a big space. She reached up, but the ceiling was too high for her to reach.

"It is not big," Prince Yester said, "Maybe t Maybe ten feet in length."

"Is there another hole on the other side?" Valda asked, "Because otherwise, there must be a way the water got in here."

She heard Prince Yester move.

"There is another hole," Prince Yester answered, "Something must have used this tunnel to escape."

"Let us go," Valda said. She moved forward.

"Okay," Prince Yester said. Then she heard him go under. When Valda reached the other wall, she took another deep breath and went under. Once again she used the sides of the tunnel to move through it. If something had used this tunnel to escape, it must have been powerful to make this tunnel.

Her lungs were starting to burn with exertion and she was still in the tunnel. Valda's mind was starting to panic when the tunnel ended and she was able to go upward. Her head broke the surface and she grabbed a lungful of air. This air was similar to the last one in the slight staleness. This was a similar space as she could stand and have her head out of the water.

This space was different from the other in that there was light in this one. It was coming from a moss growing in the space, which was stone and about ten feet in length. Another hole was visible in the opposite wall. Valda could also see Prince Yester standing there.

"It is so nice to see again," Prince Yester said.

She was not sure why, but Valda had the sudden urge to hug Prince Yester. Without any particular reason not to, Valda gave in to that urge. He was slightly surprised at first but hugged her back without thinking about it.

"It is nice to see you," Valda said.

"That too," Prince Yester said. He leaned down as she pulled back a little to look at him. Their lips met, more by accident than on purpose but still connected. The kiss sent all of Valda's nerves quivering and the whole situation disappeared from her mind. When the kiss ended, Valda stayed in Prince Yester's embrace. He did not seem to be in any hurry either. They stayed like that for several minutes.

The coldness of the water started to get to Valda and her teeth started to chatter. Prince Yester rubbed her arms, but due to them being under water it did not help.

"Let us go," Prince Yester said, "You go first."

"Okay," Valda said with a nod. She went to the hole. Taking a deep breath, Valda went under and into the tunnel. The tunnel did not have the moss growing in it, so she was left in darkness again. She pushed her way through the tunnel. As much as she could not see him, Valda could feel Prince Yester behind her.

This time Valda could feel the end of the tunnel before her lungs started to burn. Again she went upward and her head broke the surface. However, this time when she lowered the legs they did not hit bottom. She had to kick to keep herself above water. Prince Yester surfaced beside her. There was no light visible and there was no echo. It did not feel enclosed like the other areas had. In fact, there was the sound of waves on a beach coming from nearby.

"I think we have reached the open ocean," Valda said. She looked up and saw the stars. The reason it was so dark was the moon was not visible.

"I agree," Prince Yester said, "Let us head back to the island."

Valda did not have a better idea and she knew they were not done with the pirates yet. She swam behind Prince Yester as he headed for the sound of waves. It was not long before they were walking up on the beach. Valda dropped to sit in the sand. Prince Yester sat down beside her.

"It needs two locks," Valda said once she had gotten her breathing back to normal.

"There are several ways that is possible," Prince

Yester said, "But if it is in the tower, the pirates are likely to catch us again. We also have until they find out we are not trapped in the cellar."

"I hope they do not check on us in any hurry," Valda said, "Because we need to stop them and then get off the island somehow. Maybe we just need to steal the keys away from the pirates."

"How do we do that?" Prince Yester asked.

"The captain took both keys," Valda answered, "If we can get them from him, it would stop them from getting to what is locked up."

"I did not see any keys in his room when I was searching earlier," Prince Yester said, "That means he keeps them on his person. If he catches us, he will do more than just lock us away."

"So, how do we find the keys without meeting him or any of his crew?" Valda asked, "It does not seem possible."

"We will figure it out," Prince Yester answered, "Even if the way is not obvious to us right now."

Before Valda could answer, her stomach gurgled and growled. She felt her embarrassment rise in her face. Prince Yester had no choice but to hear the noises.

"I am sorry," Valda said, "But I have not eaten since the mermaids gave us that kelp."

"Then what we need to find first is some food," Prince Yester said, "I could use something to eat as well."

Prince Yester got to his feet and offered Valda a hand up. She took his hand and got to her feet. They headed towards the trees. This stretch of beach did not have any visible signs of people, so when they reached the trees there were no paths through them. Prince

Yester took the lead and went between the trees. Valda followed.

They were careful about anyone else being in the forest. It was not long before they could see the village where the pirates lived. The wooden houses appeared empty as they slowed down and got closer. But they could hear the pirates. At first it was hard to tell what was going on.

Valda followed Prince Yester out of the trees and into the village itself. No one was around. They snuck around the houses until they came within sight of a person. It was one of the pirates and he was going around a post while humming to himself. He had a mug in one hand and would take the occasional sip from it. Valda and Prince Yester stayed out of sight of the pirate, despite him not appearing to notice anything. They moved forward until they could see most of the rest of the pirates. They were gathered in the village centre, where a large bonfire burned with pirates around it. They were in various stages of being drunk.

The captain was to one side where he was seated in a throne like chair. He had a mug in his hand and was drinking from it. The rest of the pirates had their own mugs. Those who were still standing were getting more drink from one of the four barrels set up around the village centre. One was close enough to the captain he could easily dip his mug in so he could refill it.

Some of the pirates were already passed out while others worked hard to get to that point themselves. In one part of the village centre were a pair of pirates with musical instruments and they were playing while others danced or sang along. In another area, was another pirate slumped against a barrel while talking to a group sitting around listening to him. It seemed like he was telling tales.

Prince Yester tugged on Valda's sleeve and when she looked at him, he signalled for them to get away from the village centre. They were careful as they backed away. They put some rows of houses between them and the pirates before they stopped.

"Let us look in some of these houses for food," Prince Yester said, "While the pirates are distracted."

"Good idea," Valda said.

They went to the nearest house and tried to door. It was not locked. The house was barely one room and looked lived in by someone who did not mind a mess. There was no area for a kitchen and nothing that would suggest food. Nothing valuable could be seen or identified. Some of the clothing left needed more than a good cleaning and re-patching to save it.

Valda left the house and Prince Yester followed her out. He closed the door. They moved to the next house. Again the door was unlocked. Inside it was cleaner than the last house, but clothing was the main thing left. No food or valuables could be found.

"Would the food be at the tower?" Valda asked, "That main room appeared to be a dining room."

"It is possible," Prince Yester answered, "I did not see any place for cooking when I was there, but as I said I did not get the chance to search the whole thing."

"Perhaps one of the houses closer to the tower have the cooking facilities," Valda said.

"We might as well go check," Prince Yester said.

They left the house and closed the door. Prince Yester led the way around the village centre without getting too close. The pirates could be heard and they also were still busy with their drinking. Prince Yester finally led them to a row of houses close to the path that led to the tower. They started with the first house because there was no sign of any differences between the places.

The door was not locked. Inside was another residence, but this one had better furniture and more belongings. Still nothing of much value, but more comfort. It must have been the house of one of the ship's officers. However, there were still no food or kitchen facilities. Valda and Prince Yester left the house and closed the door. They went to the next house.

This time they were stopped by a lock on the door. Prince Yester started to swing and break the door, but Valda stopped him. She moved forward and popped the lock open without damaging it. Prince Yester nodded his approval before pushing the door open. This house was full of crates. Prince Yester opened a crate near the door and they looked inside. This crate had preserved food inside.

"Finally," Prince Yester said in a murmur. He took out some of the food and smelled it. Then broke it in half and offered the other half to Valda. She took it. They started eating. Valda knew better to gobble it down as much as she wanted to do that. It was better to chew it slowly as eating too fast after not eating for a while could make one sick. Prince Yester did the same.

It was not long before both had eaten enough. Prince Yester closed the crate and then they made sure to close the door when they left the house. Valda followed him to the path. They went along it until they reached the tower. No pirates were visible all along the path or outside the tower. Prince Yester opened the door and peeked in before entering. Once again, there were no pirates.

Prince Yester was about to head up the stairs, but Valda headed into the banquet room. He followed her instead. They went around the outside of the room and looking for anything that required keys. The trap door did but they already knew what was down there. When they came back around to the stairs, they went up. At the first landing, they stopped at the captain's residence. Valda went in and looked around while Prince Yester stayed outside and kept watch. She did not see anything that needed keys, but she also did not see the keys either.

Valda closed the door behind her when she left. She and Prince Yester headed up the stairs. They reached the next door and opened it. This was storage as Prince Yester had seen before. They looked through the room for anything, but they did not open any of the crates as it would have taken much more time and nothing stood out as being special. None of the crates required a key to open them. The crates took up all the space and there was no second room on this level. Again they closed the door before heading up the stairs.

The next landing did not have a door. Instead, there was no enclosed room and it was all open. There was a window beside the stairs and then another one on the other side. The space was not taken up by anything. Nothing that needed keys. It did not look like there was any reason to stop, but Valda did walk around just to check. Prince Yester waited as she did so. When she was finished, they continued up the stairs. The next landing was the last one and it had a door. The door appeared to be wooden, but it was covered with markings of someone trying to beat it down along with char marks. However, it was still solid and there were two locks in it.

"I would say that this is where the apple is locked away," Prince Yester said.

"Looks like they have not used the keys yet," Valda said, "So, we need to find the keys to keep the apple away from the pirates. The captain must have them."

"But how are we going to get them?" Prince Yester asked.

"Hopefully, a solution will present itself," Valda answered.

"I hope so," Prince Yester said, "Let us get out of this tower before we get caught."

"Good idea," Valda said.

They headed back down the stairs. They watched for pirates, but did not see any. Reaching the bottom of the tower, Valda and Prince Yester headed back along the path. When they came in sight of the houses, they left the path and went into the village. The bonfire could be seen from several rows of houses and the pirates could be heard to still be partying.

Valda and Prince Yester were careful as they got close enough to see the party. Almost everything was as they saw it last time, the difference being that a few more were passed out. The story teller was still going, but some of his audience were out. Some who had been dancing had collapsed. One was still conscious and singing, but did not appear to be able to stand up.

The captain was still in his chair with his mug in his hand. He seemed to be finding enjoyment in watching his crew and their drinking. The captain was fairly drunk himself and he was still drinking.

"Maybe we should wait until he is passed out," Valda said, "Then we should able to search his pockets."

"It might take a while," Prince Yester said, "He may not pass out at all. However, it might be our only chance."

"We need to find someplace where we are more comfortable if we need to wait for a long time," Valda said.

"Good idea," Prince Yester said.

They looked around and found a place to sit in between two houses where they could see the party but not be seen. As much as the partiers were drunk, Valda and Prince Yester did not want to take the chance of being caught again. They watched as the pirates continued to drink. Valda wondered how the pirates could not be tired and falling asleep. She could feel the activities of the day weighing her down. They put pressure on her eyelids and pushed them downward. She blinked to keep them open.

Valda was close to actually being asleep when she saw one of the pirates coming towards her and Prince Yester. She was sure they had been seen and all her muscles tensed up. Prince Yester placed a hand on her wrist to keep her from moving. They stayed frozen in place as they watched the pirate stagger closer and closer. He reached the area between houses, but moved closer to one. At first, Valda thought he had seen them and was moving to go around the house to cut them off, but then she heard the sound of liquid hitting the wood of the house.

Relief passed through Valda, followed quickly by disgust. But she and Prince Yester stayed still until the pirate staggered back to the party. She could feel the tension leave her body. Prince Yester let up on his grip but left his hand on her arm. Valda felt more alert with that scare. The pirates did not appear to be slowing down with their partying. Valda blinked again and she felt her eyelids seal before she lost herself to sleep.

"Princess Valda?" Prince Yester's voice went along with her shoulder being shaken. She opened her eyes. The sky was light. She looked over and saw the bonfire was burned down. None of the pirates were still awake. Prince Yester was already on his feet. Valda scrambled to get to her own.

Together they made their way towards the captain. They moved carefully as they did not want to disturb anyone from their sleep. Many of the pirates snored or talked in their sleep, which made Valda nervous that they would wake up. However, none of them had been disturbed by the time Valda and Prince Yester reached the captain. He was sleeping in his chair with his mug still in his hand.

Valda reached out and felt the pockets of the captain's coat. She did not feel anything there. Moving on to his vest, she tried those pockets. She did not feel the keys in those either. The captain snorted and shifted slightly causing Valda to back off. She waited several minutes as the captain did not move aside from breathing. Her hands were shaking a little, but she took a moment to settle herself before trying for the captain's pants pockets. The keys were in his left pants pocket.

To gain access Valda had to move around the captain. She had to come in from between the arm of the chair and the seat. Be careful of waking the captain and not getting her arm stuck, Valda slipped her fingers into the pocket. She managed to hook the keys with her fingers and started to draw them out. Valda could just see the tops of the keys when she froze as the captain's snorted again. When it seemed he was still asleep, Valda pulled the keys the rest of the way out of the pocket. She grasped them in her hand to prevent them from hitting each other and making noise.

Valda carefully backed away from the captain and his chair. Prince Yester went over to join her. She grabbed his hand and used that to get up on her feet. The captain snorted again, but this time he shook his head. Valda and Prince Yester did not hesitate, they started running towards the path. They did not look back but they could hear the captain shouting. It did not take long before more voices were added to the captain's voice as he woke his crew.

Valda was not sure she had ever run that fast in her life. Prince Yester stayed with her, though at times she thought he could have outrun her. She glanced briefly behind her. The pirates were yelling but they were not yet coming after them. It did not slow her down, instead, it meant she worked to keep up with Prince Yester as it was better to put as much distance as possible between them and the pirates. The path seemed to go on forever while they were running along it. Fortunately, it was daylight and Prince Yester had been along the path before, making it slightly easier.

Finally, they reached the beach and only then did they stop running. Valda kept moving forward but she worked to get her breath back. Prince Yester went to the long boats. Valda tried to keep up, but he did not seem to be getting into the boat as he pushed it into the water. Especially when he moved on to the next long boat. Valda realized what he was doing, so she went to the long boats on the other side and started pushing them into the water. The water pulled the long boats out farther.

When there was one long boat was left, Prince Yester held it long enough for Valda to get into it before pushing the long boat into the water and jumping in. Prince Yester rowed the long boat to the ship. When they reached the ship, Valda helped Prince Yester attach the long boat to the ship. Then they climbed up on deck. Prince Yester had to instruct Valda how to get the ship moving while he did everything else. Valda her best to follow his instruction, fortunately, Prince Yester used terms she understood as Valda had listened to sailors and knew there was plenty they said that she did not understand.

Together they got the ship moving away from the island. Prince Yester was dealing with the sails while he had Valda manning the tiller. She could not see precisely where they were headed, but Prince Yester had instructed her to keep going straight for now. Keeping a ship on course was a lot harder than she thought it would be as the ship tried to move one side or other rather than straight ahead. Prince Yester had to climb up into the sails to adjust them properly. She was glad she did not having to do that.

Across the water Valda could hear something, which at first she was not sure what it was but slowly realized it was the pirates shouting. She wished she could see what was happening as it sounded like the shouting was getting closer. Valda could see Prince Yester occasionally and he did not seem too rushed about anything. She wondered if that was because there was no point, or he had not noticed the pirates coming. The ship should be picking up speed, but Valda could not tell whether it was or not. Steering was not getting any easier as the tiller wanted to pull right out of her hands.

The farther they went the more Valda felt her arm muscles burn. After everything, Valda thought she could not hurt anymore, but apparently, she had been wrong. Back in Proster, Valda and Aldous had always thought adventures would be fun and their reading presented adventures as fairly fun. Back when she and Prince Yester had been swimming with mermaids, it had been much more fun. Now that they were running from pirates, it was not quite as fun, though Valda supposed that if they got back to tell the tale it might not be so bad.

"We are getting farther away from them," Prince Yester's voice interrupted Valda's thoughts.

"What?" Valda asked. She struggled to keep the tiller still.

"They grabbed one of the long boats and are coming after us on the long boat," Prince Yester answered, "They did not use it to get the other boats, but came straight after us. They have multiple people to row, but there are so many in the boat it is slowing them down. The sails are in place and I can take the tiller for a while."

Valda wanted to contribute by continuing this job, but her arms were ready to give out. She nodded. Prince Yester took the tiller from her before she let go. Valda sat down on the deck. From there she realized the ship was moving faster than she had thought it was.

"Will we get away from them?" Valda asked.

"I hope so," Prince Yester answered.

Valda waited until she thought she could move before getting up. She went to the railing and looked behind them. She had no difficulty seeing the long boat. The captain was higher than the rest of the pirates. They had four paddles for rowing, but Prince Yester was right about them being slowed down by too many in the boat. However, they did not seem to be stopping the pursuit. Valda had hoped that being on board the ship they would be safe from the pirates.

She went back over to where Prince Yester was and sat down again. She had thought about offering to take the tiller back, but she was not quite ready yet.

"How do you feel about adventures now?" Prince Yester asked. She looked at him and saw the bit of a smile.

"I think I could do without the pirates," Valda answered, "But they do not appear to be ready to do without us."

"I would have said to just throw the keys overboard and hope they would go away," Prince Yester said, "But they may be our only way of getting out alive if they get on board the ship."

"Except we do not want them to have the keys," Valda said.

"I know," Prince Yester said, "But maybe we can trick them and that is the important part. Also, how would we get rid of them?"

"The pirates do not swim," Valda said, "We would just have to throw them over the side."

"Most sailors do not swim," Prince Yester said.

"That was why they were looking for a mermaid,"

Valda said, "The keys were in a pool and they could not swim to get to them. But I am not sure a mermaid could have done it."

"Why?" Prince Yester asked.

"Because it was fresh water," Valda answered.

"You are right," Prince Yester said, "Everything I know about mermaids, they do not survive in fresh water. I may be wrong there, but I would have to ask one."

"What happened to the mermaids?" Valda asked.

"They did not want to spend too much time in this area as it contains predators that eat mermaids," Prince Yester answered, "They helped me as much as they could but then I was on my own. They will find us again if we manage to get back because they will want the stories owed."

"They did help, so they do require payment," Valda said.

"I do not want to think of their revenge if they do not," Prince Yester said.

"Do you need me to take over again?" Valda asked.

"No, I am okay for now," Prince Yester answered, "The sails do not need adjustment yet."

"Tell me when you do," Valda said.

"I will," Prince Yester said.

Valda stayed still and let her thoughts wander. She wondered how things were back in Proster. She supposed nothing quite as exciting as was happening to her. Lady Gildore was probably worried about her. Valda wondered if Yester was sending out a searching party for them, or whether the kingdom just accepted that anyone lost during the storms was truly gone. Prince Yester's stories suggested that people survived the storms all the time, but it came down to whether the stories were believed or not. He had treated them as stories until they were sitting on the island lost at sea.

"Do you think anyone is looking for us?" Valda asked.

"It is likely," Prince Yester answered, "But I do not know how long it will take before they do."

"The ship would have gotten through, right?" Valda asked.

"I hope so," Prince Yester answered, "Because otherwise, we would have seen some of the crew when we were on the islands, unless the ship was lost with all hands. Then our arrival might be the first sign of trouble."

"I hope the ship survived," Valda said.

"I do too," Prince Yester said.

Valda got up and went to the railing. She looked behind them. The long boat was farther away than last time, however, they were still coming. Being slower did not mean they were gone. Valda went back and sat down.

"They are falling behind," Valda said.

"Good," Prince Yester said, "The more distance the better."

Valda nodded as she agreed with him. They were quiet for several minutes. Then Prince Yester started to hum. Valda did not recognize the tune, but she did not mind listening to it. It was the type of song that was easy to get caught in the mind.

"Are there words to that?" Valda asked.

"Yes, but they are non-sense," Prince Yester answered, "And I do not remember them all, but I like the tune."

"I like the tune as well," Valda said.

He went back to humming it and she was quiet listening to him.

The sun was very close to the horizon when Valda realized the ship was slowing. Standing up, she looked around and realized the wind was not filling the sails as much as it had been.

"Can you take this?" Prince Yester asked.

"Yes," Valda answered. She took the tiller so he could let go. Prince Yester went to see what could be done about the sails and getting more wind. He came back far too soon.

"There is no wind to move us along," Prince Yester said.

"What do we do?" Valda asked.

"We use what momentum we have and hope it is enough," Prince Yester answered, "This ship was meant to be powered by the wind and even if there was a rowing deck, we would not be able to row with just two people."

"How much farther do we have to go before we might be safe?" Valda asked.

"What do you mean?" Prince Yester asked.

"You said that we were in an area the mermaids had predators in," Valda answered, "How far do we have before we might be in safer water?"

"Soon hopefully," Prince Yester answered, "But I really am not sure, partly because I do not know how far away we are from the safer waters. I am pretty sure we are going in the right direction to get there."

"Maybe you should go watch to see where we are," Valda said.

"Good idea," Prince Yester said. He headed for the front of the ship. Valda hoped the pirates were not getting too close as Prince Yester figured out how far to safety. If they could get to safer water, they could swim. Steering the ship still took a lot more muscle than Valda felt it should and she could feel her arms getting tired again. But Valda refused to let the ship have its way while she still could.

Prince Yester came back. He sat down where she had before. She did not ask him to take the tiller back because he looked tired.

"We are getting there," Prince Yester said, "We might be there about the time the pirates reach us."

"Is there any way to give us more time and space?" Valda asked.

"I do not think so," Prince Yester answered, "Unless you can think of something."

"Anything on board we can use?" Valda asked.

"They removed all the cargo when they landed on the island," Prince Yester answered, "I am not sure what they left that we could use. I will take over the steering and let you look."

"Okay," Valda said. Prince Yester took the tiller before Valda let go. She went below and looked around. There were some rope and a couple of cutlasses. Valda also found a musket with some balls and powder. She took those up on deck.

"Can you shoot?" Valda asked.

"I have never used a musket," Prince Yester answered, "Have you?"

"No," Valda answered, "But my father let me learn how to use a bow and it should be similar. There is a cutlass for each of us should the pirates board."

"What are you going to do?" Prince Yester asked.

"See if I can shoot a hole in their boat, if they get close enough," Valda answered.

"Good luck," Prince Yester said.

Valda took the musket, balls, and powder to the back of the ship. She lay down on the deck and peered off the stern of the ship. The long boat with the pirates was far enough behind the ship that Valda was sure she would miss if she tried shooting at them now.

Valda waited. With the ship slowing, the long boat did get closer. Valda remembered to load the musket while she was waiting. Unlike a bow, it was harder to get the target in sight. Valda did the best she could as she waited. The long boat got closer, but not quite close enough.

The ship had been slowing down and the pirates had figured that out. Since their long boat was man powered, they could keep their speed up and gain on the ship. They did not appear to be worried about anyone on the ship fighting back. Valda understood why they would feel that way as neither she nor Prince Yester had shown any sign of being fighters. She had not been in a situation with the pirates where fighting would have been worth trying and now she would be.

The long boat was now close enough Valda felt she might be able to hit them, but she held off for another moment. Then she lined up the shot with the side of the long boat and as near to the waterline as she could. Valda fired. The musket was a lot louder than she expected and she coughed at the smoke that came from the musket.

The pirates were scrambled a little at being shot at, but the captain shouted at them to keep the boat moving forward. Valda fought through the effects of being so close to the musket when firing to reload it. When it was ready, Valda lined up another shot. Once again, she aimed for the waterline of the long boat. She fired. Valda had no idea if she hit anything as the smoke in her eyes made it hard for her to see. She turned away and blinked the smoke out before turning back to reload.

When she had reloaded, Valda looked to aim and saw the pirates were settling into rowing. If they had been scrambling after that last shot, they had recovered quickly. It was easier to aim this time as the long boat was much closer. Valda figured she might have two more shots before they would be too close for her to get a proper shot. She was careful about her aim and then fired. The smoke got into her eyes and throat.

Valda reloaded the musket as she cough and blinked. She aimed the musket again and shot at the long boat. As with all the rest of the shots, Valda could not see the results of her shot. Valda reloaded the musket and aimed at the long boat. As she looked, Valda thought she saw a hole in the long boat near the waterline. She once again aimed at the long boat and hoped to get another hole in it as it would sink faster with two holes than just one.

Now the long boat was almost too close and Valda figured she would not get another shot off. She took the musket, balls, and powder with her when she returned to where Prince Yester was.

"I think I got the boat," Valda said, "But they are too close and the boat is not going to sink fast enough. How much farther did we need to get?"

"Hopefully not far," Prince Yester answered. He was

tying the tiller with the rope so the ship would not move from its current course. Just as he was finishing, they heard the pirates clamouring up the side of the ship. Valda dropped the musket and stuff down below deck. Then she and Prince Yester each grabbed a cutlass.

The captain led the pirates over the railing and towards the two. Of the six Valda had seen in the long boat, only five were coming towards them. Valda did not know why the last pirate was not with them, but she was glad there was one less they would have to fight.

"Your foolishness is going to be your undoing," the captain said, "You will not get away from us this time."

"We have the keys you are looking for," Valda said, "And we are willing to lose them in the water."

"Not if we get them for you before you have a chance to lose them," the captain said.

"Then come and get them," Valda said. She brought the cutlass to ready. Prince Yester did the same and Valda could see that he knew how to use a sword as well. The captain did not seem worried about them holding cutlasses towards his crew, who had taken out their own cutlasses. Valda and Prince Yester moved backwards toward the front of the ship as the pirates came towards them.

When the crew reached Valda and Prince Yester, there was a clash as cutlass met cutlass. The pirates appeared to be surprised that both could use the cutlasses they were holding. The biggest problem was that there were multiple pirates to each of them. However, both were good enough to hold multiple opponents back. They were not good enough to win in a fight against several opponents. They let the pirate push them back towards the front of the ship.

"Beat them already," the captain shouted at his crew, "Get those keys."

The pirates were having more trouble than they thought, but none of them could spare the time or energy to answer him. Valda and Prince Yester were blocking more attacks than actually attacking. It was enough to keep them from getting hurt. They moved closer and closer to the front of the ship and none of the pirates were worried about it as they did not seem to realize what was going on.

Valda and Prince Yester were finally backed into the railing at the front of the ship. The pirates grinned as they kept up their attacks. They thought there were winning and they had trapped the two. Suddenly the captain started shouting. This was enough of a distraction to the pirates, who could not hear what he was shouting. Valda and Prince Yester hopped over the railing and jumped into the sea below.

Valda felt her head go under and then she bobbed back to the surface. Prince Yester came up next to her. The pirates were yelling from the ship. Valda and Prince Yester started swimming away from the ship, but at a slight angle so the ship would not run over them. They could hear the pirates doing something on the ship, but they focused on getting away and not what was going on above them.

There was a splash of something hitting the water behind them. Valda glanced behind her briefly before focusing on moving forward. She had seen the net, which had caught her the first time. In her focus, Valda missed the net coming up underneath her and Prince Yester until it was almost touching them. She used the cutlass to hit the net. It did not cut through, but it did start to do some damage. Valda hit it again. Prince Yester did the same as the net was coming up around them. It took multiple hits, but they did manage to cut a hole in the net and swim through it.

They continued swimming away from the ship. The pirates started to run into the same problem Valda and Prince Yester had in that there was no wind to power the ship. Even if the net had no hole in it, they had gotten too far out for the pirates to try again. Valda and Prince Yester swam quickly as they could to get as far as they could.

GETTING AWAY FROM THE PIRATES AND GETTING HELP FROM MERMAIDS TO GET HOME

Prince Yester helped Valda up on the sand of the beach of the island. They were both tired and out of breath. Valda barely got out of the water, even with Prince Yester's help, before she collapsed. They had been swimming for a long time and barely left the pirates behind before this island appeared on the horizon. They swam for it, even though they both knew it was not far enough from the pirate ship. Prince Yester sat down in the sand beside Valda.

"There are five trees on this island," Valda said.

"There are," Prince Yester said, "I do not remember the story to go with the island with five trees."

"That is too bad," a female voice said from nearby, "We had hoped to hear another story."

Valda and Prince Yester looked over to see the mermaids floating in the water close to the island.

"I remember stories," Prince Yester said, "But I do not know the story connected to the island with five trees. I would gladly tell you another story, but I am not sure this would be a good time to stop and tell you any."

"What is wrong?" the red haired mermaid asked.

"The pirates," Prince Yester answered, "We angered them and then worked hard to get away from them. If they catch up, they will try to kill us."

"We will not get our stories if they kill you," the greenish-blond haired one said.

"There is a small ship we have seen in this area," the brunette one said.

"Did it have a crest on the sail?" Prince Yester asked.

"Yes," the brunette one answered, "It is the crest from Yester."

"That ship will help us," Prince Yester said, "And might actually be searching for us. Where is it now?"

"Over there," the greenish-blond one answered pointing off into the distance where there was nothing visible on the horizon.

"How far?" Prince Yester asked.

"Kilometres," the greenish-blond one answered.

"But it is going in the wrong direction," the brunette said.

"Then we need a way to get there," Prince Yester said.

"How far to the next island?" Valda asked.

"A swim," the greenish-blond one answered.

"Maybe we should go there and then figure out how to get to the ship," Valda said, "Then we will be safer from the pirates and will have time to think."

"Good idea," Prince Yester said, "Can you help us get to the next island?"

"Certainly," the brunette answered.

"Maybe we can get a story at the next island," the red-haired one said.

"This way," the brunette said.

Valda and Prince Yester went into the water. As soon as they were in the water, the mermaids started to swim. The two followed the mermaids.

A swim turned into several hours of swimming. It tired the two out further but they kept going. When they reached the next island, Valda and Prince Yester moved far enough up to not be in the water and then collapsed there.

"Why would the ship be searching for you?" the brunette asked, "Many have been lost at sea but those of Yester never send out ships to look for them."

"Because they want their prince back," Valda answered.

"You are the Prince of Yester?" the brunette asked.

"Yes," Prince Yester answered.

All three mermaids disappeared under the water and were gone.

"What was that about?" Valda asked.

"I am not sure," Prince Yester answered, "But I hope it is good news because I cannot move again today."

"I am with you there," Valda said, "I feel too tired to move."

She reached out for his hand and he took her hand in his. Then Valda closed her eyes and let herself sleep.

Valda rolled over and found herself sleeping on the sand with her hand in Prince Yester's hand. She stayed still as she suddenly did not want to move. The sun was between the horizon and its height, but she could not tell whether it was going up or going down. The sounds of splashing caused Valda to sit up enough to look. The mermaids were in the water.

"We brought the ship," the brunette said, "It is coming."

"Thank you for directing the ship to us," Valda said.

"We had to," the greenish-blond one said, "Without the officials from Yester, we mermaids would be endangered by overfishing. They may not always remember, but we do. The pirate ship has been misdirected and is not likely to find you again."

"Thank you," Valda said.

"The captain said you were a princess," the red-haired one said.

"I am Princess Valda of Proster," Valda said.

"Oh, you are from Proster?" the greenish-blond one asked.

"You have heard for Proster?" Valda asked.

"Sure, there were some issues helped by King Proster," the red-haired one answered, "His sword sliced through the monster that would not leave us alone. The officials from Yester did not have a weapon strong enough to work. King Proster did not even get mad at us when he lost one of his men."

"King Proster was used to battle and used to losing men in fights," Valda said, "He fought plenty of monsters."

"The man was not lost in battle," the red-haired one said with a giggle, "He was lost to a mermaid."

"That happens?" Valda asked.

"You think we only lose mermaids to men?" the

greenish-blond one asked.

"I have only heard a few stories about mermaids and most of them are that way," Valda answered, "But I suppose it makes sense that it goes both ways. Some stories have mermaids drowning men who fall for them."

"Those are not mermaids," the red-haired one said, "Those are sirens and their goal is to sing men to their deaths. We do not do that. We like to help people."

"We appreciate your help with everything," Valda said.

"We have to go," the brunette said, "You will tell him about the ship?"

"I will," Valda answered, "If you come find us again, he will tell you the stories we owe you."

"You do not owe us anything," the brunette said.

"Then it is an offer if you want," Valda said.

"Thank you," the brunette said. The mermaids went under and Valda saw the one's tail as they swam off.

Valda was not sure what to do now, so she just sat there. Prince Yester remained asleep. She did not want to wake him up until she had to. The sun moved slightly higher into the sky. Valda felt Prince Yester release her hand. He moved it up to his head and used the palm of his hand to rub his eye.

"We need to figure out how to get to the ship," Prince Yester said.

"Not really," Valda said.

"How are we going to get there otherwise?" Prince Yester asked.

"Maybe they will row the long boats over to the island," Valda answered.

"What do you mean?" Prince Yester asked. He sat

up.

"It is coming this way," Valda said before pointing it out on the horizon. Prince Yester looked and saw the ship.

"I guess we wait then," Prince Yester said, "I wonder how they found us."

"The mermaids," Valda said, "They stopped by the island earlier and said they told the ship where to find us. They said they had to help you out because officials of Yester helped out mermaids. I told them you would still tell them the stories if they want and they said you did not owe them stories anymore. I left the offer for them anyway."

"It is good of them to help us," Prince Yester said, "And of course, I will tell them more stories. Did they mention the pirates?"

"Yes," Valda said, "They said they had misdirected the pirates."

"Good to know," Prince Yester said.

They sat there and watched the ship get closer and closer. The ship did have the Yester's crest on the main sail. When the ship reached shallow water, they put a couple long boats in the water. One of the men on the long boats appeared to be the captain of the ship and was wearing a uniform with the Yester's crest on it. The long boats reached the sand and the man stepped out while the rest stayed in the boats.

"Prince Yester and Princess Valda?" the captain asked.

"Yes," Prince Yester answered while Valda nodded.

"It is great to find you," the captain said with a sigh of relief, "We were getting worried we would not find you two. Let us get on the ship and back to the kingdom."

"We would appreciate that," Prince Yester said.

The captain helped Valda into the long boat and Prince Yester got in followed by the captain. The boats pushed off and were rowed back to the ship. Once there, Valda and Prince Yester were helped on board before the sailors pulled the boats up.

"Princess Valda!" was the only warning before Lady Gildore hugged Valda.

"I was so worried that we would have to return to Proster with the message that you were lost," Lady Gildore said.

"I had hoped we would be found before anything happened," Valda said.

"But your dress," Lady Gildore said.

"We had to swim," Valda said, "And I could not do so with my dress."

"Understandable," Lady Gildore said, "I have one of your dresses in my bags." Lady Gildore pulled Valda towards the cabins area. Valda looked back and saw Prince Yester's chaperone looking after Prince Yester, though it did not look like Prince Yester was enjoying it.

Lady Gildore had a whole outfit for Valda, who was happy to change into fresh clothing. When Valda was refreshed, Lady Gildore had some water and food for Valda. She sat down and slowly enjoyed the food and drink.

"I told the king you were not likely to want to return to Proster, if we found you," Lady Gildore said, "That you had fallen in love with Prince Yester. Was I wrong?"

"You are not," Valda said, "I want to stay, if Prince Yester wants me to stay."

"He has already asked if you are okay since you went to change," Lady Gildore said, "I believe he wants you to stay. You will like Yester when you get to see it. The captain said it will only take a couple days to get back."

"I cannot wait to see it," Valda said. Lady Gildore smiled before going back to her needlework.

After she was finished eating, Valda went up on deck. She found Prince Yester leaning against the railing. He smiled at her and she smiled back. Prince Yester had been given a clean outfit and appeared to have washed as well.

"For an adventure, it was not too bad," Valda said, "Though several times during it, it was not so fun."

"I think that is how adventures go," Prince Yester said, "It is not so bad when it over, but it is not comfortable during it. The captain said we were going to be in Yester in a couple days."

"Lady Gildore said as much," Valda said, "She also said she told the king that I likely would not be interested in heading back to Proster."

"She was right," Prince Yester said.

"She was," Valda said. Valda reached into her pocket and took out the two keys. She offered them to Prince Yester. He took them and held them in his hand. Then he offered one back and she took it.

"To remind us of everything," Prince Yester said.

"It does seem fitting," Valda said with a smile. She put her key back in her pocket. He put his away.

"I am going to have to ask my mother about mermaids," Prince Yester said, "See what kind of stories they like."

"The mermaids said they knew King Proster," Valda said.

"You will have to tell me about him," Prince Yester said.

"I am not as good a story teller as you are," Valda said.

"Does not matter," Prince Yester said, "If I am supposed to tell you stories, you can tell me some. No one else has to hear you tell stories."

Valda smiled at him and felt like she had found where she belonged in life.

There was a slight fluttering in Valda's stomach as she and Prince Yester stood in front of the large doors leading to the throne room where the king and queen of Yester were waiting. As much as Valda loved Prince Yester and as much as she knew he loved her, she was still nervous about meeting his parents. The guards opened the door and Prince Yester escorted her inside. The throne room was large and their footsteps echoed in the space. It was intimating, even to someone who had spent her life in a castle.

Sitting on a raised dais in two thrones were the king and queen. Both of them had crowns of gold and jewels as well as outfits of expensive fabrics. Valda felt completely underdressed and out of place. The queen was willowy and elflike in her movements. The king was medium height and a little pudgy around the middle as if age was starting to catch up with him.

"Ernest!" the queen got to her feet and went down the steps from the throne. Prince Yester let go of Valda so he could hug his mother.

"We were worried we had lost you to the sea," the queen said.

"I am sorry to cause you to worry," Prince Yester said, "And I would like you to introduce you to Prince Valda of Proster."

The queen turned to Valda and smiled at her.

"It is so nice to meet you," the queen said holding out her hand.

"You too," Valda said letting the queen have her hand. The queen's hands were soft and warm and the queen gave off a feeling of comfort that Valda almost forgot to curtsy. The king had also come down from the dais.

"Lady Gildore believed you would stay and become part of the family," the king said.

"That is the plan, if you would let me," Valda said.

"Of course, we will let you," the king said, "We welcome you and hope you find Yester your home."

"It has been so far," Valda said, "And I cannot wait until to see the rest and get to know the people."

"Wonderful!" the queen said, "Will Lady Gildore being staying as well? She seemed to have an interest in one of our older nobleman."

"She told me that she wants to stay," Valda said, "And will only return to Proster if I send her. I will not do so unless there is a good reason."

"There are no good reasons to send her away," the queen said, "I am sure you will want someone from home around for the wedding as we do not know any traditions from Proster."

"Lady Gildore likely knows more about them than I do," Valda said.

"Well, we will have to sit down and have a long

discussion with her soon," the queen said. She put her arm around Valda's shoulders and started to direct out of the room.

"But we will welcome you to the family with a delicious supper," the queen said.

"That sounds delightful," the king said.

"After a few days lost at sea, supper sounds wonderful," Prince Yester said.

They headed for the door of the throne room. Valda felt more than welcome to the kingdom of Yester and the royal family. On the side the queen was not holding, Valda reached back for Prince Yester's hand. He took her hand in his and squeezed it.

THE END?

"Fascinating," Thompson said, "But has nothing to do with history."

"I am not sure about that," Mitchell said, "The next one may change your mind about that."

"Why are you so set on believing these books have anything to do with history?" Thompson asked, "The only thing it is going to do is cause trouble."

"You know I have not always trusted what others tell me," Mitchell answered, "And these books might prove they are lying."

"Are you sure?" Thompson asked.

"Here, listen to this," Mitchell answered. He picked up the next book and started to read it out loud.

ABOUT THE AUTHOR

Heather Mantler is a lover of fairy tales and fables. Her home town is Prince George, British Columbia. Heather is always working on another story as she hopes to finish every story idea that she has ever written down. She was a nominee for the fiction category of the 2012 Prince George Regional Arts and Cultural Awards and short listed for the 2013 John Harris Fiction Awards. Her blog is heathersdomain.wordpress.com. Heather encourages her readers to post reviews on Good Reads and Amazon.

www.ingramcontent.com/pod-product-compliance
Lightning Source LLC
Chambersburg PA
CBHW051512170626
46811CB00002B/783